HE SAID, SIDHE SAID

ALSO BY TANYA HUFF

THE BLOOD BOOKS

Blood Price
Blood Trail
Blood Lines
Blood Pact
Blood Debt

THE SMOKE BOOKS

Smoke and Shadows
Smoke and Mirrors
Smoke and Ashes

THE QUARTERS NOVELS

Sing the Four Quarters*
Fifth Quarter*
No Quarter*
The Quartered Sea*

THE KEEPER CHRONICLES

Summon the Keeper
The Second Summoning
Long Hot Summoning

TORIN KERR NOVELS
Valor Novels

*Valor's Choice^*
*The Better Part of Valor^*
Heart of Valor
Valor's Trial
The Truth of Valor

Peacekeeper Novels

An Ancient Peace

THE ENCHANTMENT EMPORIUM

The Enchantment Emporium
The Wild Ways
The Future Falls

WIZARD OF THE GROVE

The Last Wizard
Child of Light
Wizard of the Grove (omnibus)

STANDALONES

The Fire's Stone*
Gate of Darkness, Circle of Light*
The Silvered

SHORT STORY COLLECTIONS

What Ho, Magic!
Stealing Magic
Relative Magic
Finding Magic
Nights of the Round Table*
February Thaw*
Swan's Braid, and other tales of Terizan*
He Said, Sidhe Said*
Third Time Lucky*

*available as a Jabberwocky ebook
^also available in the omnibus A Confederation of Valor

HE SAID, SIDHE SAID

AN ANTHOLOGY BY

TANYA HUFF

Published by JABberwocky Literary Agency, Inc.

He Said, Sidhe Said

Copyright © 2013 by Tanya Huff

All rights reserved.

First published as an ebook in 2013 by
Jabberwocky Literary Agency, Inc.

This edition published in 2016 by JABberwocky Literary Agency, Inc.

1. A Choice of Endings
originally published in MAIDEN, MATRON, CRONE, DAW
    Books Inc., 2005 and collected in Finding Magic, ISFIC Press,
    2007

2. Finding Marcus
originally published in SIRIUS THE DOG STAR, DAW Books
    Inc., 2004 and collected in Finding Magic, ISFIC Press, 2007

3. He Said, Sidhe Said
originally published in FAERIE TALES, DAW Books Inc., 2004
    and collected in Finding Magic, ISFIC Press, 2007

4. I'll Be Home for Christmas
originally published in THE CHRISTMAS BEASTIARY, DAW
    Books Inc., 1992 and collected in What Ho, Magic, Meisha
    Merlin, 1999

5. Tuesday Evenings, Six Thirty To Seven
originally published in EERIECON CHAPBOOK, 2006 and
    collected in Finding Magic, ISFIC Press, 2007

6. Under Summons
originally published in MythSprings, Fitzhenry and Whiteside,
    2006 and collected in Finding Magic, ISFIC Press, 2007

7. Word of Honour
originally published in TALES OF THE KNIGHTS TEMPLAR,
    Warner, 1995 and collected in What Ho, Magic, Meisha Mer-
    lin, 1999

Cover design by Tara O'Shea

Interior design by Estelle Leora Malmed

ISBN 9781625672018

TABLE OF CONTENTS

A Choice of Endings • 1

Finding Marcus • 21

He Said, Sidhe Said • 43

I'll Be Home for Christmas • 67

Tuesday Evenings, Six Thirty To Seven • 95

Under Summons • 123

Word of Honour • 153

Mrs. Ruth first appeared in my 1989 novel, *Gate of Darkness, Circle of Light*, as avatar of the Crone. She's cranky and pragmatic and gave voice to one my favourite bits of dialogue. In answer to an Adept of the Light telling a frightened young man, *"Your scar is a Warrior's mark. Wear it proudly."* Mrs. Ruth replied, *"What bloody help is that? Prompt medical attention and it may not scar at all."*

I kind of love Mrs. Ruth a lot. When invited into an anthology called *Maiden, Matron, Crone* (I have no idea why they chose to use Matron not Mother), I promptly pulled Mrs. Ruth out of retirement.

The year I wrote this story, a child was abducted out of her home in the Annex in the middle of the night by someone who broke in and drugged her to keep her quiet. Years later, I can't remember how things ended for the child, but I have a niggling sense it wasn't good. At the time, this was the only thing I could do about it...

A CHOICE OF ENDINGS

When the phone in the elderly and filthy phone booth began to ring, several people who were part of the morning rush heading for the Spadina subway station jumped. The incessant 24/7 warble of cell phones from pockets and purses hadn't prepared them for the strident and insistent ring of old technology. A couple of the older commuters moved to pick up—their responses set in a childhood when such a ring demanded immediate attention. One after another, they changed their minds upon reaching the booth. Perhaps it was the prevalent scent of urine or a perfectly valid fear of catching something virulent from the grimy receiver or the sudden certain knowledge that the call couldn't possibly be for them.

And the phone rang on.

"All right, all right, I'm coming. Don't get your damned panties in a twist!" An elderly woman, dressed in several layers of grimy clothing, pushed a heavily loaded shopping cart along the crowded sidewalk, scattering pedestrians like pigeons. Although collisions seemed unavoidable, no collisions occurred. A heavily perfumed young woman did snap one heel off a pair of expensive shoes after making an observation about street people and personal hygiene and asylums, but that was probably a coincidence.

Possibly a coincidence.

Actually, not likely to be coincidence at all.

The shopping cart finally parked by the booth, a gnarled hand, gnawed fingernails surprisingly clean, picked up the receiver.

The ringing stopped.

The sudden silence turned heads.

"What?"

And the city dweller's innate ability to ignore the poor, the crazy, and most rules of common courtesy turned heads away again.

The voice on the other end of the phone was pleasantly modulated, genderless, and just a little smug. "Mrs. Ruth, this is your third and final warning. The power is about to pass. Please see that your affairs are in order."

Mrs. Ruth, the eldest avatar of the triple Goddess, She who was age and wisdom and kept council during the dark of the moon, slammed the receiver back down onto the phone, coughed for a while, spat a large gob of greenish-yellow phlegm onto the stained concrete, and snarled, "Bite me."

She'd known her time was ending for months now. It was, after all, what she did. What she was. She knew things. She knew the name of every pigeon who'd lost its home when the university tore down Varsity Stadium. She knew the hidden places and the small lives that lived in them. She knew the pattern of the larger lives that filled the city with joy and laughter and fear and pain. She knew that something was going to happen only she could prevent and she bloody well wasn't going anywhere until it did and she had.

"They can come and get me if they want me to go that badly!" she told a passing driver as she crossed Bloor Street against the lights, deftly moving her cart through the places the cars weren't. The driver *may* have questioned how he could hear her, given that his windows were up, his air conditioning was turned on, and he was singing along with a Justin Timberlake CD his daughter had left in the car, but she didn't stop to find out if he had. Another day she would have; questions were her stock in trade. Today, she didn't have time.

The trouble with knowing things was that not everything known was pleasant. There had always been dark places in the pattern; she acknowledged them, kept an eye on them, and, when her help was requested, assisted in removing them.

When her help was requested. That was the sticking point.

"I can't just go fixing things willy nilly," she pointed out to a young man jogging past.

Without really knowing why, he slowed and asked, "Why not?"

"Well, what will you learn from that?" Mrs. Ruth responded. "That I can fix things?" She blew a moist raspberry. "You have to learn to fix things yourself. I'm just a tool in the great toolbox of life."

"But what if you can't fix that… thing on your own? What if you've tried and it stays unfixed?"

"Ah, then you have to learn just who to ask for help. Your parents have been married for what, twenty-nine years?"

"Yeah, but…"

"You think that maybe they know a thing or two about staying together?"

"My parents have always said they won't interfere in my life."

"Uh huh."

"So, I should ask them…?"

"Ask them what they had to do to make their relationship work." Which was, quite possibly, the most direct answer she'd given in thirty years.

"But…"

Not that it seemed to matter. "Just ask them, bubba."

He frowned at her then and reached into his belt pouch. "Power bar?"

"Sure."

And off he jogged, feeling good about himself because of a little effortless charity. He'd already forgotten the conversation, but that didn't matter. The things he'd needed to know that he already knew now lay along the surface of his thoughts where they'd do him some good.

Mrs. Ruth snorted as she watched him jog away. Time was, she could have spun her answers out for blocks, switching between allegory and insult at will. No one appreciated words of wisdom that seemed to arrive too easily. Trouble with common sense was folks had stopped appreciating anything considered *common*. Granted, they'd stopped some time between coming out of the trees and walking erect, but it still pissed her off.

Time was…

Time wasn't. That was the problem.

The wheel of life turned. Sometimes, it ran over a few hearts on the way. As a rule, her job was to remind folk that there wasn't a damned thing they could do about it.

"Why did this happen to me?"

"Because."

"It's not fair!"

"No, it isn't."

"How can I stop this?"

"You can't."

But she could. It was within her power to change the pattern—if she could just hang on to that power long enough. She was *not* having her end and this particular bit of darkness coincide.

"I'm not denying that it's time," she muttered at her reflection. "There are days I feel more tired than wise."

Her reflection, keeping pace in the windows of parked cars, snorted. "Then let go."

"No. I can't let it happen again."

"You can't stop it from happening again, you old fool."

Mrs. Ruth sighed and raised a hand to rub at watering eyes. That was true enough where *it* referred to the general rather than the specific. But she could stop this particular *it* from happening and she was going to.

With only one hand guiding it, the shopping cart twisted sideways and slammed into the side of a royal blue sedan. The car alarm screamed out a protest.

"Oh, shut-up!"

The alarm emitted one final, somewhat sulky, *bleep* then fell silent.

Shaking her head, Mrs. Ruth dug into the depths of the cart, shoving aside old newspapers, her entire wardrobe except for the blue socks which she'd left hanging on the bushes by the church, and eighteen faded grocery bags filled with empty Girl Guide cookie boxes and bottles of Tabasco sauce. Down near the top half of the 1989 Yellow Pages, she found a coupon for complimentary body work at Del's Garage on Davenport Road at Ossington. Del had played high school football with the owner of the car and was about to be in desperate need of a good lawyer. The owner of the car had married a very good lawyer.

"There." She shoved it under the windshield wipers. "Two for one. Don't say I never did nothing for you. And stop staring at me!"

Her reflection suddenly became very interested in getting a bit of secret sauce off the sleeve of her shapeless black sweater.

Frowning slightly, Mrs. Ruth laid her palm against the warm curve of glass and wondered when her joints had grown so prominent, her fingers so thin. She remembered her hands fat and dimpled. "You look old," she said softly.

Under the crown of her messy grey braid, the lines on her reflection's face rearranged themselves into a sad smile. "So do you."

"You look older!"

"Do not!"

"Do too!"

"Excuse me, are you all right?"

Mrs. Ruth turned toward the young woman standing more than a careful arm's length away—compassion's distance in the city. "When he asks you how you did it, tell him it's a secret. Trust me; things'll go a lot better if he never knows."

Or had that already happened? Past and future threads had become twisted together.

And why was she speaking Korean when the girl was clearly Vietnamese?

"No! Not now!" Her hands closed around the bar of her shopping cart and she closed her eyes to better see the fraying threads of her power and draw them back to her. Through force of will she rewove the connections. Breathing heavily—a moment later or ten, she had no idea—she opened her eyes to see the young woman still standing there but clearly ready to run. "I'm fine," she told her through clenched teeth. "Really, I'm fine."

With no choice but to believe, the girl nodded and walked quickly away.

On the corner of College and Spadina, a phone began to ring.

"I will repeat this only one more time," Mrs. Ruth growled in its general direction. "Bite. Me. Mange. Moi."

People moved out of her way as she hobbled toward the Eaton Centre. Most of her scowl came from the pain of a cracked tooth caused by all the clenching. Most.

In nice weather, he ate lunch on a bench outside the north end of the Centre where he watched small children roll past in strollers or dangle from the hands of hurrying adults. These children were too young, but he enjoyed speculating on how they would grow. This one would suddenly be all legs, awkward and graceful simultaneously, like a colt. That one would be husky well into his teens when suddenly his height would catch up with his weight. Her hair would darken. His dimples would be lost. After his sandwich, his apple, and his diet cola, he'd go back into the store and later, when school was out, he'd help the parents of older children buy expensive clothing, clothing the child would grow out of or grow tired of long before they'd gotten their money's worth from the piece. The store had a customer appreciation program—every five hundred dollars spent entered the child's name in a draw for the latest high-tech wonder. Names and ages and addresses were collected in a secure data base. Where secure meant accessible only by store staff.

She knew all this when she lowered herself down beside him on the bench and arranged the layers of her stained black skirts over her aching legs. "I won't let it happen, bubba."

Knowing what he knew, hiding what he hid, he should have asked, "Let what happen?" and that question would have given her a part of him. Every question she drew out after that would have given her a little more. It was how conversations worked and conversations could be directed. Direct the conversation, direct the person having it.

But he said only, "All right."

White noise. Nothing given.

"Everyone has limits. I've reached mine."

He said, "Okay." Then he folded his sandwich bag and slid it into his pocket.

Her presence used to be enough to make them open up.

Today, holding on to her power by will alone, not even leading statements were enough. Should she release enough power to draw him to her, she'd lose it all before she had time to deal with what he was.

He stepped on his empty diet cola can, compressing it neatly. Then he scooped it up and stood.

Mrs. Ruth stood as well.

He smiled.

His smile said, as clearly as if he'd spoken aloud, *"You can't stop me."*

A subconscious statement he had no idea he was making.

"Oh right! You're a big man facing down an old lady! I ought to run over your toes until you can't walk!" He looked startled by her volume, admittedly impressive for a woman her age. More startled still when she grabbed his sleeve. "How'd you like a little Tabasco sauce where the sun don't shine!"

"Okay, that's enough." The police constable's large hand closed around her wrist and gently moved her hand back to her side. Fine. Let the law handle it. Except she couldn't just tell him what she knew, he had to ask.

She glared up at him. "Never eat anything with mayo out of a dumpster—all kinds of evil things hiding in that bland whiteness."

She was hoping for: "What the hell are you talking about?"

Or even: "Say what?"

But all she got was: "Words to live by, I'm sure. Now, move along and stop bothering people."

Over her years on the street she'd met most of Toronto's finest—a great many of them even were—but this big young man with the bright blue eyes, she didn't know. "Move along?

Move along? Listen, bubba, I owned these streets while you were still hanging off your mother's tit!"

"Hey!" A big finger waved good naturedly at her. "Leave my mother out of this."

"Your mother…" No, better not go there. "I can't leave yet. I have something to do."

When the bright blue eyes narrowed, Mrs. Ruth realized she'd been speaking Hungarian. She hadn't spoken Hungarian since she was nine. The power was unravelling again. By the time she wove things back into a semblance of normalcy, the cop was gone, *he* was gone, she was sitting alone on the bench, and the sun was low in the sky.

"Shit!"

She had no time to find a Hero, and the other Aspects were too far away even if they'd agree to help. Which they wouldn't. The Goddess was a part of what kept this world balanced between the light and the dark. She was the fulcrum on which the balance depended. Should the balance shift in either direction, Her Aspects would come together to right it, but this… this evil was nothing unusual. Not dark enough to tip the scales and with light enough in the world to balance it.

"Business as per bloody usual."

And all very well if only the big picture got considered. One thing the years had taught her—her, not the Goddess— was that the big picture didn't mean bupkes to those caught by the particulars.

Getting a good grip on her shopping cart, Mrs. Ruth heaved herself up onto her feet. She could still see to the point where the dark pattern intersected with her life although she no longer had strength enough to see further. Fine. If she followed the weft to that place, she'd have one more chance.

"The Gods help those who help themselves."

Laughing made her cough, but, hell, without a sense of humour she might as well already be dead, so, laughing and coughing, she slowly pushed her cart north on Yonge Street. She couldn't move quickly but neither could she be stopped.

"After all," she told two young women swaying past on too-high heels, "I am inevitable."

The elder of the two paled. The younger merely sniffed and tossed pale curls.

That made her laugh harder.

Cough harder.

Phones rang as she passed, handing off booth to booth, south to north like an electronic relay.

At Yonge and Irwin, a middle-aged woman held her chirping cell phone up under frosted curls, frowned, and swept a puzzled gaze over the others also waiting for traffic to clear. When Mrs. Ruth pushed between an elderly Asian man and a girl with a silver teardrop tattooed on one cheek, her eyes cleared. She took a step forward as the cart bounced off the curb—boxes rattling, newspapers rustling—and held out her phone.

"It's for you."

Mrs. Ruth snorted. "Take a message."

"They say it's important."

"Do they? What makes their important more important than mine?" When the woman began to frown again, she rolled her eyes. "Hand it over."

The phone lay ludicrously small on her palm. She folded her fingers carefully around it and lifted what she hoped was the right end to her mouth. "She has to pay for this call, you inconsiderate bastards." Then she handed the bit of metal and plastic back and said, "Hang up."

"But…"

"Do it."

She used as little power as she could, but enough had been diverted that she lost another thread or two or three… Breathing heavily, she tightened her grasp on those remaining.

At Bloor Street she crossed to the north side and turned west, moving more slowly now, her feet and legs beginning to swell, the taste of old pennies in the back of her throat.

"Could be worse," she found the breath to mutter as she approached Bay Street. "Could be out in the suburbs."

"Could be raining," rasped a voice from a under a sewer grate.

She nodded down at bright eyes. "Could be."

From behind the glass that held them in the museum, the stone temple guardians watched her pass. Fortunately, the traffic passing between them was still heavy enough, in spite of the deepening night, that she could ignore their concern.

By the time she reached Spadina, more and more of her weight was on the cart. When the phone at the station began to ring, she shot a look toward it so redolent with threat that it hiccoughed once and fell silent.

"Right back where… I started from." Panting she wrestled the cart off the curb, sneered at a streetcar, and defied gravity to climb the curb on the other side. "Should've just spent the day… sitting in the… sun."

By the time she turned north on Brunswick, the streets were nearly empty, the rush of people when restaurants and bars closed down already dissipated. How had it taken her so long to walk three short blocks? Had she stopped? She couldn't remember stopping.

Couldn't remember…

Remember…

"Oh no, you don't!" Snarling, she yanked the power back. "When. I. Choose."

Overhead, small black shapes that weren't squirrels ran along the wires, in and out of the dappled darkness thrown by the canopies of ancient trees.

"Elderly trees," she snorted. "Nothing ancient in this part of the world but me."

"You're upsetting the balance."

She stared down at the little man in the red cap perched on the edge of her cart, twisting the cap off one of the bottles of Tabasco sauce. "Not so much it can't be set right the moment I'm gone. Trust me…" Her brief bark of laughter held no mirth. "…I know things."

"You're supposed to be gone *now*," he pointed out, and took a long drink.

"So?"

That clearly wasn't the answer he'd been expecting. "So… you're not."

"And they say Hobs aren't the smartest littles in the deck."

"Who says?"

"You know." She thought she could risk taking one hand off the cart handle long enough to gesture. She was wrong. The cart moved one way. She moved the other.

"You're bleeding." The Hob squatted beside her and wrinkled his nose.

"No shit." Left knee. Right palm. Concrete was much

tougher than old skin stretched translucent thin over bone. She wouldn't have made it back to her feet without the Hob's help. Like most of the littles, he was a lot stronger than he appeared and he propped her up until she could get both sets of fingers locked around the shopping cart handle once again. "Thanks."

He shrugged. "It seems important to you."

She didn't see him leave, but it was often that way with the grey folk who moved between the dark and light. She missed his company, however brief it had been, and found herself standing at the corner of Brunswick and Wells wondering why she was there.

The night swam in and out of focus.

Halfway down the block, a door closed quietly.

Her thread…

His thread…

Mrs. Ruth staggered forward, clutching the pattern so tightly she began to lose her grip on the power. She could feel her will spread out over the day, stretched taut behind her from the first phone call to this moment.

This moment. The moment her part of the pattern crossed his.

A shadow reached the sidewalk in the middle of the block, a still form draped over one shoulder. The shadow, the still form, and her. No one else on the street. No one peering down out of a darkened window. A light on in the next block—too far.

This was the reason she'd stayed.

The world roared in her ears as she reached him. Roared, and as she clutched desperately at the fraying edges, departed.

He turned. Looked at her over the flannel-covered curve of the child he carried.

It took a certain kind of man to break silently into a house, to walk silently through darkened halls to the room of a sleeping child and to carry that child away, drugged to sleep more deeply still. The kind of man who knew how to weigh risk.

She was falling. Moments passing between one heartbeat and the next. Her power had passed. She was no risk to him.

He smiled.

His smile said, as clearly as if he'd spoken aloud, *"You can't stop me."*

It was funny how she could see his smile when she could see so little else.

Then he turned to carry the child to his car.

As the sidewalk rose up to slap against her, curiously yielding, Mrs. Ruth threw out an arm, and with all she had left, with the last strength of one dying old woman who was no more and no less than that, she shoved the cart into his heel.

Few things hurt worse than a heavily laden shopping cart suddenly slamming into unprotected bone. He stumbled, tripped, fell forward. His head slammed into the car he'd parked behind, bone impacting with impact resistant door.

The car alarm shrieked.

Up and down the street, cars joined in the chorus.

"Thief! Thief! Thief!"

Their vocabulary was a little limited, she thought muzzily, but their hearts were in the right place.

Lights came on.

Light.

Go into the light.

"In a minute." Mrs. Ruth brushed off the front of her black sweater, pleased to feel familiar substantial curves under her hand, and watched with broad satisfaction as doors opened and one after another the child's neighbours emerged to check on their cars.

Cars had alarms, children didn't. She frowned. Should have done something about that when she still had the time.

He stood. A little dazed, he shoved the shopping cart out of his way. Designed to barely remain upright at the best of times, the cart toppled sideways and crashed to the concrete, spilling black cloth, empty boxes, and bottles of Tabasco sauce. One bottle bounced and broke as it hit the pavement a second time directly in front of the child's face. The fumes cut through the drug and she cried.

He started to run then, but he didn't get far. The city was on edge, it said so in the papers. These particular representatives of the city were more than happy to take out their fear on so obvious a target.

The Crone is wisdom. Knowledge. She advises. She teaches. She is not permitted to interfere.

"She didn't. I did. The power passed before I acted. I merely used the power to get to the right place at the right time. No rules against that."

You knew that would happen.

Not exactly a question. Mrs. Ruth answered it anyway. "Nope, I'd had it. Reached my limit. I had every intention of blasting the son of a bitch right out of his Italian loafers. Fortunately for the balance of power, I died."

The silence that followed filled with the sound of approaching sirens.

But the cart...

"Carts are tricksy things, bubba. Fall over if you so much as look at them wrong."

And the Tabasco sauce?

"What? There's rules against condiments now?"

You are a very irritating person.

"Thank you." She frowned as her body was lifted onto a stretcher. "I really let myself go there at the end."

Does it matter?

"I suppose not. I was never a vain woman."

You were cranky, surly, irritable, self-righteous, annoying, and generally bad tempered.

"But not vain."

The child remained wrapped in her mother's arms as the paramedic examined her. The drugs had kept her from being frightened and now she looked sleepy and confused. Her mother looked terrified enough for both of them.

"They'll hold her especially tightly now, cherish each moment. When she gets older, she'll find their concern suffocating, but she'll come through her teenage rebellions okay because the one thing she'll never doubt will be her family's love. She'll have a good life, if not a great one, and the threads of that life will weave in and about a thousand other lives that never would have known her if not for tonight."

The power has passed. You can't know all that.

Mrs. Ruth snorted. "You really are an idiot, aren't you? She pulled a pair of sunglasses from the pocket of her voluminous skirt and put them on. "All right, I'm ready. Life goes on."

But you knew it would.

"Not the point, bubba." She turned at the edge of the light for one last look. It wasn't, if she said so herself, a bad ending.

Okay, I am not a dog person. I like dogs—better than I like most people—but I'm not one of those people that forms bonds with dogs. My wife is. Our dogs adore her. They follow her from room to room, their ears perk up at every single passing car when she's out, and they throw themselves on her when she comes home. They obey me and they like me well enough, but they don't love me. On the other hand, there are usually three cats on my side of the bed for most of the night. Sometimes four.

So, writing a story for an anthology called *Sirius the Dog Star* was a bit of a challenge. Rising to that challenge, I decided I wouldn't merely write about dogs, I'd be the dog. In a literary sense.

Plus, I don't much like first person point of view. I find it limiting. (I'm not saying it *is* limiting, I'm saying that's how I find it.) There are only a few authors who write in first person that I read and out of twenty-eight books and seventy plus short stories, I've written first person point of view three times. *Finding Marcus* was the second time.

Also, I've never been asked to be in one of the many cat anthologies. I find that interesting, although, admittedly, not exactly relevant to the matter at hand...

FINDING MARCUS

The rat was fat, a successful forager, over-confident. It had no idea I was hunting it until my teeth closed over the back of its neck and, by then, it was far too late. As I ate, I gave thanks, as I always did, that some bitch in my ancestry had mated with a terrier. If I'd been all herder or tracker, I'd have been long dead by now. A puddle from the recent rains quenched my thirst and, with my immediate needs satisfied, I took a look around.

The Gate had dumped me in an alley, pungent with the smell of rotting garbage, shit, and stagnant water. There were other rats in the big overflowing bins, roaches under everything, and a dead bird somewhere close. The bins were metal. Never a good sign.

I lifted my head to the breeze coming in from the distant mouth of the alley and sighed. Cars. It's a scent you don't forget. Mid-tech world at least. Although I could already feel the pull of the next Gate, it'd be harder to find it in the stink of too many people and too much going on. Still, it wasn't like I had much of a choice.

And sometimes the low-tech worlds were worse. A lot worse. Fear and suspicion on a low-tech world had separated us…

Before I left, I marked the place where the old Gate had been. Not so I could find it again—they only worked in one direction—it's something I've done ever since I got into this mess, a way of saying that the Gates are mine, not the other way around. And besides, sometimes I just need to piss on the damn things.

I had a quick roll in the bird as I passed. A guy's got to do some stuff for himself.

At the mouth of the alley, I felt a slight pull to the left so I turned. Nose to the ground, I could smell nothing but the rain. The sky must have cleared just before I showed up. Marcus could be mere minutes ahead of me and I'd never know it.

Suddenly regretting the rat, I started to run.

Marcus could be mere minutes ahead of me.

Minutes.

By the time I stopped running, I'd left the alley far behind. I knew I wouldn't catch up to him so easily, but sometimes it takes me that way, the thought that he could be close, and my legs take over from my brain. I always feel kind of stupid afterward. Stupid and sad. And tired. Not leg tired; heart tired.

The pull from the next Gate hadn't gotten any stronger so I still had a distance to travel. I had to cross a big water once. Long story. Long, wet, nasty story.

The made-stone that covered the ground was cleaner here. Smelled more of people and less of garbage, although I hadn't yet reached an area where people actually lived. At a corner joining two large roads, I lifted my head and sniffed the sky. No scent of morning. Good. It had been nearly mid-dark when I'd entered the Gate one world back, but time changed as the worlds did and I could have lost the night. Lost my best time to travel, lost my chance of catching up to Marcus.

I dove back into a patch of deep shadow as three cars passed in quick succession. Most of the time, the people in cars were blind to the world outside their metal cages, but occasionally on a mid-tech world, a car would stop and the people spill out, bound and determined to help a poor lost dog. I was hungry enough, hurt enough, stupid enough to let them once.

Only once. I barely escaped with my balls.

When the road was clear, I raced across, and though it made my guts twist to ignore the path I needed to follow, I turned left, heading for the mouth of a dark alley. Heading away from the lights on poles and the lights on building, away from too much light to be safe.

The alley put me back on the path. When it ended in a dark canyon between two buildings, I turned left again, finally spilling out onto another road; a darker road, lined with tall houses. I could follow this road for a while. The lights on the poles were further apart here, and massive trees threw shadows dark enough to hide a dozen of me.

As it happened, the shadows also hid half a dozen cats.

Cats are contradictions as far as I'm concerned; soft and sweet and harmless appearing little furballs who make no effort to hide the fact that they kill for fun and can curse in language that would make a rat blush. I took the full brunt of their vocabulary as I ran by. Another place, another night, and I might have treed a couple, but with the Gate so far away, I needed to cover some serious distance before dawn.

Sunrise found me running along a road between houses so large they could almost be called palaces. Probably a rich merchant area. High-tech, mid-tech, low-tech—some things never changed. People who suddenly found themselves with a lot of stuff had to show it off. Marcus, who never had anything except me and a blithe belief in his own intellect, used to laugh about it. He used to laugh about a lot of things. He wasn't laughing when they tore us apart; he was screaming my name, and that's how I remember him most often.

I couldn't stay on this road much longer, it was beginning to curve away from the direction I needed. But first, breakfast.

Low-tech, high-tech; both were essentially garbage free. But mid-tech—when they weren't piling it in metal bins, people in mid-tech worlds actually collected their garbage up into bags and set it out in front of their houses. It was like they were bragging about how much they could waste. A guy could eat well off that bragging.

Second bag I ripped open, I hit the jackpot. A half-circle of flat bread with sausage and cheese crumbled onto a sauce. I gulped it down, licked the last bit of sweet cream out of a container, and took off at full speed as a door opened and a high-pitched voice started to yell.

Over time, I've gotten good at knowing when I'm not wanted.

As I rounded the curve at full speed, I saw that the houses had disappeared from one side of the road. In their place, a ravine—wild and overgrown and the way I needed to go. The spirit pack was definitely looking out for me on this world, but then, by my calculations, I was about due. I jumped the barrier and dove through the underbrush.

A squirrel exploded out of the leaf litter in front of me, and I snapped without thinking. It managed half a surprised squeal before it died. Carrying it, I made my way down the steep bank, across a path at the bottom, and halfway up the other side. Someone, a long time ago by the smell of it, had scratched out a shallow den under the shelter of a large bush. I shoved my kill between two branches because I don't like the taste of ants and, if I got lucky, off the ground would keep them off the squirrel. Although, it *was* sort of comforting that ants tasted the same on every world. Food safe, I marked the territory as mine and made myself comfortable.

Down on the path, a female person ran by. Nothing seemed to be chasing her. Running beside her was a lovely black and white bitch with pointed ears and a plumy tail. She glanced up toward me as she crossed my trail, flattened her ears, but kept running, clearly aware of where her responsibilities lay. I could appreciate that. Chin resting on my front paws, I went to sleep.

The heat of the sun warm on my fur when I woke told me I'd been asleep for a while. The question: what had woken me? The answer: a sound. A rustling in the bush above me. When I heard it again, I slowly opened my eyes.

A small crow sidled toward my squirrel. Only half the size of some crows I'd seen, its weight was still enough to shake the branch. With one claw raised, it glanced toward me and froze.

"Nice doggy. There's a nice, big doggy. Crow not tasty. Doggy not eat crow."

"I hadn't intended to," I told her, lifting my head. "But I don't intend to allow you to hop in here and eat my kill either."

The crow blinked and put her raised foot down. "Well, you're a lot more articulate than most," she said. "Practically polysyllabic." Head to one side, she took a closer look. "I don't think I know your breed."

"I don't think you do," I agreed. "I'm not from around here."

Left eye, then right eye, she raked me up and down with a speculative gaze. "No, I don't imagine you are. You want to talk about it?"

"No." She took flight as I crawled from the den, but after a long, luxurious scratch, I realized she'd only flown up into the nearest tree. "What?"

"Where's your… what is it you dogs call them again? Your pack?"

I'd have howled except that was a good way to attract the kind of attention I didn't want. Marcus had been the only pack I'd ever had.

"Is that what you're looking for?"

"What makes you think I'm looking for anything," I growled.

"Well, you're not from around here. So…" She hopped along the branch. "…I'm wondering what you're doing here. You're not lost—you lot are so obvious when you're lost—therefore, you're looking for something. Someone." Crows always looked pleased with themselves, but something in my reaction shot her right up into smug and self-satisfied. "I knew it. You have a story."

"Everyone has a story." I started up the bank.

"Hey! Dog! Your squirrel."

"You can have it." Anything to keep her from following me. It didn't work. I heard her wings beat against the air then she landed on a jutting rock just up the path. I don't know why people call cats curious. Next to crows, they're models of restraint.

"Sometimes, it helps to share."

I drew my lips back off my teeth. "Sometimes, I like a little poultry when I first wake up."

"Poultry!" They probably heard her indignant shriek on the other side of the Gate. "Fine. Then I'm not going to warn you that the roads are full and you'll never get anywhere unseen. They'll grab you and stuff you into a cage so fast, it'll make your tail curl!"

I nearly got whacked on the nose with a wing as I passed. At the top of the ravine, I peered out between two metal poles and realized the crow had been right. This was another place where no one lived, and the roads were full of cars and people.

I marked both posts, hoping that, given enough time, the crow would have flown off, then I started back to the den.

"I told you so."

She was still there. But, on the bright side, so was my squirrel.

"Look, dog, maybe we got off on the wrong foot. Paw. Whatever. You're on your own and that's not the usual thing with you lot and I'm on my own and that's not so usual for my lot either. You're probably lonely. I'm not doing anything right now. You've got a story and I'd love to hear it. What do you say?"

I bit the tail off my squirrel's fat little rump, spat it to one side, and sighed. "Do you have a name?"

"Dark Dawn With Thunder."

I blinked. "You're kidding?"

She shrugged, wings rising and falling. "You can call me Dawn."

"Rueben." With one paw holding down the squirrel's head, I ripped the belly open and spilled the guts onto the ground. "Here. You might as well eat while you're listening."

"So you'll tell me your story?"

"Why not. Like you said, you're not going away." Neither was I. Talking over the pull of the Gate might help keep me from doing the truly stupid and risking the roads. I'd never find Marcus if I was locked in a cage. And I *was* lonely. Not that I'd admit as much to a crow. "So…" I swallowed the last of the squirrel and sat down in the shade. "…what do you know about the Gates between the worlds?"

I expected to startle her. I didn't.

She tossed back a bit of intestine. "I know what all crows know. I know they exist. I know the way of opening them has been lost for a hundred thousand memories."

"It's been found again."

"You came through a Gate?"

"And I'm leaving through one."

"You don't say." She searched the ground for any bit she might have missed then folded her wings and settled. "Start at the beginning…"

"Marcus."

My beginning. Hopefully, my end.

I'd been with him ever since I'd left my mother's teat and the warm comfort of my litter-mates. I remember falling over my feet as I chased a sunbeam around his workshop. I remember becoming too big for his lap and sitting instead with my head resting on his knee. I remember the way his fingers always found exactly the right place to scratch. I remember how he smelled, how he sounded. I remember the first Gate.

I think he wanted to prove himself to the old ones in his pack. They believed he was too young to do anything of merit, but he only laughed and carried on. He talked to me all the time about what he was doing; I only wish I'd understood more. But understanding came later when, unfortunately, he had a lot less time to talk.

I don't know how he found the Gate. I don't know how he opened it, although there were candles lit and a lot of weeds burning and copper wires and a thunderstorm. I'm not embarrassed to admit I yelped when the lightening hit. Marcus laughed and rubbed behind my ears, the sound of my name in his mouth comforting. Then he took hold of the fur on the back of my neck and we walked forward.

Every hair on my body stood on end, and for a heartbeat light, sound, and smell vanished. If not for the touch of his hand, I would have bolted. When the world came back, it was different.

The sun was low in the sky—it had been mid-light mere moments before—and we stood on a vast, empty plain. No buildings. No smoke. No sign of his pack.

He was happy. He danced around and I danced with him, barking.

And then we found out we couldn't get home.

The Gates only worked one way.

I found the next Gate. And the next. By the fourth world, Marcus had learned to sense their pull—and that was a good thing, because it was the first mid-tech world we'd hit and I was in an almost constant state of panic.

By the fifth, I realized that all sounds he made had meaning. The Gates were changing me. I remember the first thing he said that I truly understood.

"Well, Rueben, old boy. Looks like we'll have to keep going forward until we get home."

Only the first Gate—the Gate on the world where you belong—fights against being opened. After that, it seems to be merely a matter of knowing where they are. They recognize you don't belong, and the next thing you know it's a brand new world. Those first five worlds, when it was just me and Marcus, surviving by our wits, working together, depending on each other's skills the way a pack is supposed to, those were the happiest times of my life.

The sixth world was low-tech and we emerged into a crowded market place. Marcus staggered a little, steadying himself on my shoulder. By the time he straightened, the crowds had begun to scream, "Demon!" I didn't know what it meant, but I knew anger and fear when I heard it, when I smelled it, so I braced my front legs and growled.

Marcus tried to soothe me. He thought that laughter and intellect would win the day, but I knew he was wrong. If they were going to take him, they'd have to go through me.

I didn't know about crossbows then.

I learned.

It took three to knock me off my feet, but I was still snapping and snarling as they dragged us away and threw us in a tiny, stinking, dark hole to wait for the priest.

Marcus begged cloth and water and herbs from the guards.

He kept me clean, he kept me alive. I don't know how he convinced them to part with such things, but that was when he stopped laughing.

I think he'd begun to realize how much I understood, because there were things he didn't talk about.

The priest finally came.

The priests in Marcus' old pack were always good for a bit of something sweet and an absentminded scratch. This was a different kind of priest. The smell of anger clung to him like smoke.

They dragged us out, blinking and squinting in the sunlight. Marcus lifted his face to the sky like he'd forgotten what it looked like, like he'd been afraid he'd never see it again. They said we were demons and demons had to die. The priest told us we would burn on top of a holy hill so the smoke would rise into the demon worlds and warn others of our kind to stay away. He said a lot of other things too, but none of it made any more sense, so I stopped listening.

As we walked to the pyre, I stayed pressed close against Marcus' legs because I think he would have fallen if I hadn't been there. Not that I was in much better shape.

Then we got lucky.

At the top of the hill, I felt a familiar pull, and I knew from the noise Marcus made low in his throat that he felt it too. The Gate. And it was close. On the other side of the hill, about halfway down. We should have been able to feel it all along, but I think that whatever made the hill holy had blocked it. I didn't think that then, of course, but I do now.

The way things had been set up, there wasn't room for more than one man to hold Marcus as he climbed onto the pile of wood. Why would they need more than one? He was so thin and in so much pain, and even I could see that all our time in the darkness had broken something in him. When he wrenched himself free, they froze in astonishment. He grabbed the single rope they had around my neck and we ran.

They hadn't thought we had the strength to escape, you see. They were right.

They caught us at the Gate. We'd gotten so close that it had opened, and they held us so close that it stayed open, waiting for us to leave a world where we didn't belong. Bleeding from new wounds, Marcus tried to explain. The priest refused to listen. He knew what he knew, and nothing anyone could say would change that. As they began to drag us away, I saw my chance and sank my teeth into the arm of the man who held me. He screamed, let me go, and I threw my entire weight against Marcus' chest, pushing him and the man who held him back into the Gate. We could deal with *him* on the other side.

Then a hand grabbed the end of the rope tied around my throat and hauled me back.

Marcus screamed my name and reached for me, but he was falling too fast. He was gone before my front paws hit the ground.

If the priest thought I'd waste my strength throwing it against the rope, he was

very wrong. I took most of his hand through the Gate with me. It took me two worlds to get the taste out of my mouth.

The crow hopped along the branch and stared down at me, head cocked. "So you got away?"

"Obviously."

"Where's Marcus? Wasn't he waiting for you on the other side of the Gate?"

"No." I scrubbed at my muzzle with both front paws to keep myself from howling. "I found out later that you have to be touching for the Gate to send two lives to the same world."

"You're looking for him."

It wasn't a question, but I answered it anyway. "I don't know if he's still by that Gate waiting for me to come through or if he's on his way around trying to get back to that world again, but, yes, I'm looking for him."

"How long?"

Rolling onto my side, I licked a fall of fur back off an old, faded scar. "This was where one of the crossbow bolts hit. It was open and bleeding when Marcus was thrown through the Gate."

Dawn glided down beside me and peered at my side. If crows knew anything at all, they knew wounds. "A long time."

"Yes. But I *will* find him."

She nodded. "I don't doubt you'll keep trying. It's a dog thing. Hopeless…"

My growl was completely involuntary.

"Hopeless," she repeated, clacking her beak. "But romantic. You're lucky crows are a lot more practical."

"Lucky?"

"Because you shared your story, I'm going to help you get to your Gate."

Before I could protest, she took wing, flying toward the upper edge of the ravine. By the time I'd scrambled to my feet and shaken my fur into some semblance of order, she was back. "I don't need your help," I told her, walking stiff-legged past her position. "I can find the Gate on my own."

"I don't doubt it. But do you know what traffic is doing? Can you find the fastest route through the buildings? Do you know when it's safe to move on?" She stared at me thoughtfully—it might have been thoughtful, it might have been disdainful, it was impossible to tell with crows. "No one will notice me, but, if you're not very careful, they'll certainly notice you. Do you have a bear in your ancestry or something?"

"No."

"Pony?"

"No!"

"Marcus fiddle with your DNA?"

"My what?"

She flew ahead and landed on the guard rail. "Not important. What is important though, is that, if you hurry, you'll be able to get across the road."

I gave poultry another quick thought then leapt the guard rail.

"Run fast, dog. The light is changing."

Into what? Not important. I started to run. Metal shrieked against metal. As I reached the far side, something big passed so close to my tail that I clamped it tight between my legs and lengthened my stride. Racing along the narrow passage between two buildings, I wondered just what I thought I was doing, listening to a crow.

"You're going to come out into a parking lot. Cross it on a bit of an angle... Go to your left. No, your other left. ...and you can use the dumpster to go over the fence."

And why was I *still* listening to the crow?

On the other side of the fence, two cats hissed insults as I went by, and a small, fat dog on a rope started barking furiously. I was gone before anyone came out to investigate the disturbance, but not so far gone that I couldn't hear them blame the whole noisy situation on the cats. Pretty funny.

Determining this new road went in essentially the right direction, I stopped running full out and dropped into a distance eating trot.

"Aren't you in a hurry?" The crow was on one of the wires that crossed over the street, calling the question down to me. Not exactly unnoticeable to my mind, but what did I know of this world? "Shouldn't you be moving faster?"

"I know what I'm doing," I snapped. "Don't you have a flock to join?"

"A murder." She flew ahead and landed again.

"A what?"

"A group of crows is called a murder. A murder of crows."

"Why?" I couldn't stop myself from asking even though I knew any interest would only encourage her to hang around.

Fly ahead. Land. "I don't know."

"I thought crows remembered everything?"

Dawn shrugged philosophically. "Can't remember what I've never been told."

"All right. Fine. Don't you have a murder to join?"

Fly ahead. Land. "Not any more. I left because I'd heard all their stories."

"Stories? What does that have to do…"

She clacked her beak. "I get bored easily."

We went on like that until nearly full dark. Dawn flapped from wire to wire, telling me way more crow stories than any dog would ever want to know. A lot of them involved carrion. Then, as the last of the light disappeared, I looked up and she was gone. I shouldn't have been surprised; like most birds, crows prefer not to fly at night. Maybe she should have thought about that before she offered to help. I shouldn't have missed her. But I did.

I walked most of the night, napping twice but not feeling safe enough to sleep deeply. As the sky began to lighten, the pull of the Gate became so strong that I knew I was close. Using Dawn's dumpster trick, I went over another fence, finding Marcus the only thought in my mind.

Which was why I didn't notice the men until I was in the midst of them.

"Holy fuck! Would you look at the size of that mutt!"

They were all around me. Something hard hit me on the left shoulder, and I reacted without thinking. The scent of so many males was too strong a challenge. I whirled to the left, flattened my ears, and snarled.

The man scrambled back. I could smell his fear. A piece of broken brick glanced off my back. The sharp end of a stick jabbed at my haunches. I should have kept running. Should have. Didn't. Now they'd closed in. Too close.

I heard a length of chain hiss past my head.

If they wanted a fight…

Then I heard a hoarse shriek of outrage, a scream of pain, and the circle made up of legs and boots and rough weapons opened.

"Where the fuck did that crow come from!"

I don't know how much damage she stayed to do, but when she found me again, I'd gone to ground. I heard the sound of claws on gravel, looked out from behind the huge wheel on the trailer that sheltered me, and there she was. She snatched up a discarded piece of sugared bread, threw back her head and swallowed, then hopped closer.

"All right, I'm convinced, you really *do* need to find this Marcus of yours because you shouldn't be running around without a keeper. What kind of an idiot picks a fight with seven big, burly, cranky, construction workers before they've had their first coffee? You know, if you'd tried the *roll-over look at me I'm so cute* schtick, you'd have probably gotten a belly rub and a couple of sandwiches. Those kind of guys usually like a dog that's big enough they're not afraid of breaking it. So, you hiding under there?"

As she'd actually paused, I assumed she wanted an answer. "Yes."

"Why?"

I glanced up at the massive trailer. "Because I fit. And because the Gate's in that building."

Dawn turned enough to study the building with her right eye.

It was constructed of the big, made-stone blocks. I'd seen windows and a door along the front, but neither on the sides. The back of the building, where the trailers were parked, had a set of huge double doors and one smaller one with a light over it.

"So, what do you do now?" she asked.

"I wait." This close to the Gate, I was too jumpy to lie down, but there wasn't enough head room to pace. I had to settle for digging a trench in the gravel with a front paw. "I wait until one of those doors open, then I run inside."

"And once you're inside?"

"I keep from being grabbed long enough to get through the Gate."

"I like a dog with a plan. But I'm warning you, it's barely daylight and not a lot of people are up at this…"

One of the big double doors swung open and slammed back against the made-stone wall with a crash loud enough to fling Dawn into the air and raise the hackles on my neck. With the barrier out of the way, the pull of the Gate nearly dragged me out of my hiding place, but I'd been stupid once this morning, and stupid wouldn't help me find Marcus.

Then the other door opened and men appeared carrying huge made-things of metal and plastic and glass that I didn't recognize. I felt the trailer above me shake as they climbed up the ramp.

"Hey, a film crew." Dawn was back on the ground. "I'll let you in on a secret, Rueben—there's good pickings in the garbage outside the craft services truck. These guys never seem to have time to finish eating anything."

I had no idea what she was talking about. Nor did I care.

Two of the men were in the trailer. The other two were out of sight in the building.

My chance.

Marcus.

I was running full out by the time I reached the doors. I leapt a cart just inside, smelled the sudden rush of fear from the man pushing it, scrambled along a cloth path on the floor, skidded through a room with only three walls, found myself outside but not outside, ignored the yelling, and concentrated on finding the Gate. I'd been in buildings before—once, on a high-tech world, I'd been chased through an underground structure so complicated ants couldn't have found their way around—but nothing in this building made sense! The ceiling was too high, the walls didn't reach it, and there were cables everywhere.

I couldn't find the Gate.

My toenails scrabbling for purchase against a polished stone floor, I raced around a corner and ended up in a long hall. Three men ran toward me from the other end, one of them carrying a net. They were all making soothing sounds, the one with the net repeating, "It's okay, boy. It's okay, boy." I wanted to believe them. I wanted to lay my head on someone's knee and have him tell me I was home.

I knocked over a row of chairs, jumped a pile of cable, and ran up a flight of stairs. The stairs ended in another railing and a door. I threw myself against it.

The wall shook.

The Gate... the Gate was on the other side!

I threw myself against the door again. Someone was whining. I had a horrible suspicion it was me.

So close...

Then suddenly, the wall gave way, the stairs shook, and I jumped.

A hand closed around my tail.

The Gate opened.

I braced myself for the pain of my tail being yanked free but it never came. Instead, the grip released and sharp points of pain dug into my back.

This time the Gate dumped me on the edge of a meadow. The sun was shining, birds were singing, and I could smell both rabbits and water on the breeze. My stomach growled and I growled with it.

Ready to move on, I turned to piss on the weed growing

closest to where the old Gate had been and discovered I wasn't alone. There was a crow in the grass, lying in a parody of a nest, wings spread and feet in the air. Bending my head, I snuffled her breast feathers. Warm. Alive. The sharp pains in my back suddenly made sense.

Dark Dawn With Thunder had hitched a ride.

I glanced across the meadow, then back at her, then sighed and scratched.

I was napping when she finally came to, but the sound of her flapping awkwardly onto her feet woke me. Her wings looked as though the edges were unravelling and she staggered three paces forward then three paces back before she caught her balance.

"Rather remarkably like flying into a hydro wire," she muttered, caught sight of me, and stilled. "Nice doggie. Doggie no yell at crow. Crow have very big headache."

"Crow deserves very big headache," I told her. "What were you thinking?"

Dawn cocked her head and studied me for a moment. "I was thinking you hadn't thanked me for saving your furry ass."

She was right, I hadn't. "Thank you."

"And I was thinking that I'd like to know how the story ends."

"Story?"

"You and Marcus."

"Why do you care?"

"Care?" Twisting around, she poked her tail feathers into alignment. "I don't care. I just hate to leave a story hanging. Gives me that unfinished feeling."

I chewed a bit on a paw and when I looked up, Dawn was watching me.

"I was also thinking," she said, "that dogs are hopeless romantics and you need taking care of. And besides…" Her eyes glittered. "…you're certainly not boring."

"You can't go back," I reminded her.

"I'm not going any where until the story ends." She clacked her beak and launched herself into the air. "So, let's get a move on."

I sat and watched her fly for a moment, then smiled and shook my head. She was going the wrong way. Not that it mattered, she'd learn to feel the Gates soon enough. For now, she had me. I shook, walked out of the cloud of shed fur, and trotted across the meadow.

After a moment, I heard her wings in the air above my head.

"Any sign of him?" she called as she swooped by.

"Not yet."

The pull of the next Gate was no more than a suggestion, so we had a way to travel still and Marcus could be anywhere along the path.

I could tell the crow how the story was going to end.

I *would* find him.

But I supposed it wouldn't hurt to have a little company along the way.

It is impossible to find a skateboarding magazine in January in a small town in Canada. Snowboarding, yes. Skateboarding, no. Yet another reason why I give thanks daily for the internet. Some years after I wrote this story, the local skateboarders finished up a long and unexpectedly successful fund-raising campaign, and built a skate park in our very small town. It was more an accident of vacant land than a plan that it was built almost right next to the hospital.

Sooner or later, most fantasy writers will take a crack at re-imagining the oldest tales and *He Said, Sidhe Said* is my take on *Tam Lin*. While I think it's a fun story even if you don't know the original, it's a lot more fun if you do. And, as much as I believe this is one of the cleverest stories I've ever written, I have the nagging feeling that I owe *someone* an apology.

HE SAID, SIDHE SAID

Last summer, they built this new skateboard park down by Carterhaugh Pond; a decent half pipe, some good bowls, a pyramid, couple of heights of rails. Blatant attempt to keep us off the streets, to control the ride, but they put some thought into the design and I've gotta admit that sometimes I can appreciate a chance to skate without being hassled. It was October 24th, early morning, and I had the place to myself. Kids were all in school, and a touch of frost in the air was keeping the usual riders away.

I was grabbing some great air off the pipe and I was seriously *in* the moment, so I figured this was the time to try a backside tailslide on the lip. Yeah, yeah, there's harder tricks, but for some reason, me and tailslides... So, I picked up some serious speed, hit the lip, held the lip, and then WHAM! I was ass over head and kissing concrete.

World kind of went away for a minute or two—you know, like it does—and when I finally got my eyes open, I was staring up at this total babe. I was like, "Woo! Liv Tyler!" only without that whole kind of creepy *I look like the lead singer for Aerosmith* vibe.

Over the sound of The Bedrockers still jamming in my phones, she said, "Give me your hand!"

I figured she was going to help me up, so I put my hand in hers, and next thing I knew, the park was gone, the pipe was gone, hell, the whole world was gone. Good thing my other hand was locked on my board.

The land between the water and the wood has always been ours, one of the rare places where our world touches that of mortal men. The news that it had been defiled came to the High Court with a Loireag who dwelled in the pond. She was a plaintive little thing, wailing and keening as she made her way through my knights and ladies to throw herself damply before me.

The wailing and keening made it difficult to hear her complaint, but, eventually, she calmed enough to be understood. Great instruments of steel and sound were scraping away the earth, crushing and tearing all that was green, driving terrified creatures from their homes and into hiding.

We do not concern ourselves with the world of men, and, in return, we expect that which is ours to be respected. Clearly, it was time again to remind them of this.

When I arrived with those of my court I trusted most, I saw that the tale of woe spun to me by the Loireag was true. A great scar had been gouged into the earth and men surrounded it. Large men. Their skins browned by the sun and made damp by their labours. Cloth of blue stretched over muscular thighs, and, as I watched, one threw off a gauntlet of leather and tilted back his head to drink.

A lifted finger and I directed a spilled rivulet of water over his chest and down a ridged stomach until it disappeared behind...

"Majesty?"

I breathed deeply. "It is overly warm in the world of men," I said as a breeze sped to cool my brow at my command. "We will go and return again another day."

But our days are not the days of men, and when we returned, the scar in the earth had been filled with stone sculpted into strange and impossible shapes. In stone cupped into half a moon, a young man rode a winged board.

His hair was dark, but tipped with light, his eyes the grey-green of a storm. Loose clothing hid his body from my sight, but his hands were large and strong and he moved like water down a mountain side. His smile spoke of earthy joys.

I stepped forward as his head hit the stone.

"Not *again*, Majesty..."

Who of my court dared to voice so weary a warning, I did not know. For the sake of so enchanting a creature, I disregarded it and crossed into the world of men. Admiring the broad shoulders and lean length of my fallen hero, I reached out to him.

"Take my hand," I said.

And he did.

❖

I woke up in what I later learn is called a bower—it was kind of like a bedroom without walls, just this billowy curtainy stuff, and I wasn't alone. The babe who wasn't Liv Tyler was with me, we were both totally without clothes, and she was studying this major scabbage I've got all down my right forearm.

"Screwed up a 180 out of an axle stall," I explained, trying to sound like this sort of thing happened to me all the time—naked with a strange babe not the scabbage, because, you know, sometimes you bail.

She touched it with one finger, all sympathetic.

I probably should have been more freaked, but she was naked and I was naked and so...

It was a fast ride, but no one did any complaining.

Later, we were lying all wrapped up and worn out when this tall, skinny blonde fem wearing a lot of swishy green just wandered in without so much as a *"Hey, coming through!"*

"Majesty, your husband has sent an emissary. Will you receive him?"

"An emissary?" she asked.

Me, I was kind of fixating on a different word, although I totally kept my cool. "You have a husband?"

Once I had him unclothed, I was a little disconcerted to discover that he was damaged. His shins were an overlapping mix of purple and blue, and his right arm had been horribly disfigured.

He muttered words I did not understand, but I could feel his terror so I touched his arm to calm his fears. His reaction to my touch was unexpected. It had been long since a mortal man had shared my bed, and I had forgotten just how impulsive they are. And how quick.

About to suggest a second attempt, my words were halted by the appearance of Niam of the Golden Hair. "Majesty, your husband has sent an emissary. Will you receive him?"

About to ask who my husband had sent this time, my words were once again halted.

The mortal threw himself from the bed, hiding his manhood behind a handful of fabric. "Husband?! Oh man, you never said you had a husband!"

As he was the only man in our lands, I had no idea who he was speaking to and would have demanded an accounting had I not caught sight of that infernal Puck hanging about at the edge of hearing. He wore his usual condescending smile that told quite clearly how he would enjoy informing my Lord Oberon of my latest dalliance.

I could hear him now, insinuating that any discontent I felt was a result of my own choices.

As I would not give him the satisfaction, I bound my mortal lover round with cobwebs and as he lay silent and unmoving said, "Tell good Robin that I will speak with him anon. I have matters here to attend to still."

Niam raised a quizzical brow toward the mortal, but bowed and left as commanded, sweeping Puck before her.

I drew the mortal back to the bed and released his bindings. "You need not fear my husband," I told him. "The King has his own Court and does not come to mine."

Now, having heard *husband*, I hadn't paid a lot of attention to the rest of what the blonde chick had said. I mean, I was cool, totally dignified, but a little stunned, you know? I couldn't think of anything to say until we were alone again and the babe was trying to explain about how they were separated and I didn't have anything to worry about.

"He's the King?"

"Yes."

"And that would make you…?"

"The Queen."

Of the Fairies as it turns out. No, not those kinds of fairies. Real Fairies. Like in fairy tales. We got dressed and she lead me out onto this balcony tree-branch thing and, well, it was pretty damned clear I wasn't in Kansas anymore, if you know what I mean.

I just did the Queen of the Fairies. Prime!

"What do I call you?" I asked, tearing my eyes away from a whole section of tree that would make a wild ride.

"Majesty."

I knew she was just teasing, so I gave her my best *you and me, we're closer than that* smile. "Sure, but you got a name?"

She looked at me for a long moment, then she smiled and I knew I had her. "I am also called Tatiania."

"Annie."

"Tatiania!"

"Not to me, babe." I laid my fist against my heart. "Tommy Lane. But I tag with Teal, so you want to call me that, I'm cool with it. You know, TL… Teal."

"I think I will call you Tommy Lane," I told him. Not that it mattered; he would not be in my realm for very much longer. I would send him home the moment I had dealt with Puck.

"So while you're seeing the dude your old man sent, you mind if I ride?"

As I had no real idea of what he was talking about, I told him I did not.

He raced back into my bower and emerged with his wheeled board—it had merely seemed to have wings, so quickly had it moved. Balanced on the edge of my balcony, he grinned with such joy that I felt my heart soften toward him. Then he placed the pieces of sponge upon his ears again and threw himself forward, bellowing out a most impertinent question as he raced along the branch.

"Who's your daddy!"

With any luck, he would fall and break his neck and save me the walk back to the place where our lands touched.

"I can't wait for the feast!"

"What feast?" I snapped as Puck dropped down beside me. His manner of perching and appearing and making himself free of my Court as though it were my husband's was most annoying.

"The feast you'll be having for your skater-boy."

Tommy Lane was no longer in sight, but I could still hear the rasp of his wheels against the tree and the shriek of my ladies as he roared through bower after bower. How unfortunate that none would risk my wrath and stop his ride upon their blade. Birds took wing all around us, protesting so rude a disturbance.

"It's traditional," Puck continued, grinning insolently. "A mortal crosses over, and we throw him a feast. You can't send him back without one, not unless you made a mistake bringing him here in the first place."

Oh, he would *like* to go to my husband and say I had made a mistake. They would laugh together over it.

"Moth, Cobweb, Mustard Seed!"

The sprites appeared.

"See that a feast is made ready." As they vanished, I turned to Puck and said, as graciously as I was able, "You will stay, of course."

Wise enough to recognize the command, he bowed gracefully. "I wouldn't miss it, Majesty."

After the feast, he would go to my Lord Oberon and tell my husband of the great joy and pleasure I took in my mortal companion, and then my lord could feel the bite of being replaced once again.

I have no idea where the room came from. One minute I was having the wildest ride of my life and the next I'm landing an ollie on marble floors. I knew it was marble because Philly used to have this great park with marble slabs that was prime loc for street skating. Anyway, there were banners hanging from the ceiling and tables all down the middle and these little people laying out plates and stuff.

I saw my Annie up ahead, standing with some short brown dude—not a brother but brown; hard to explain—and so, pushing mongo-foot, I made my way over. Just before I reached her, I decided to show off a bit and so did a quick grind along the last of the marble benches that were up against the wall. Kid's trick, but she didn't ride and I could tell she was impressed.

His *board* left a black mark along the edge of the bench, and only the presence of my husband's emissary kept me from freezing his blood on the spot.

❀

Flashing my sharpest smile, I planted one on right on the royal lips. "Hey, babe, what up?"

❀

I did not have the words…

Mostly, because I hadn't understood the question, but also because of his fearless stupidity. This was truly why we find mortal men so fascinating. Not content merely to die, they spend their short lives courting death in so very many ways. And, in truth, the salutation was a bit distracting.

"He wants to know what's going on," Puck said helpfully.

I ignored him and graced my unwelcome paramour with my full attention. "My people prepare a feast in your honour, my love. Rich raiment befitting one who shares my bower has been laid out for you. Go and adorn yourself in silk and velvet."

"Silk and velvet? Not my deal. I appreciate the thought, but I'm cool."

"You will be warmer in the clothing that has been made ready for you."

He threw back his head and laughed and, to my horror, wrapped an arm around my waist and pulled me tightly against his side. I would have turned him into a newt then and there if not for the irritatingly superior smile on the face of Robin Goodfellow.

"Isn't my Annie the greatest?" Tommy Lane declared once he had his laughter under control.

Puck bowed deeply so that I could not see his expression. "She is indeed," he said.

The food was great. A little poncy, you know, with sauces and garnishes and fancy stuff, but there was lots of it, and it tasted prime. Unfortunately, the after dinner entertainment of one guy with Spock-ears and a harp, totally sucked. I had to ask what the harp was; I thought maybe it was some kind of warped axe. Oh, and the dude was blind, but he was no Stevie Wonder. I figured they were all being so nice to him because he was blind, and that was cool, but the piece he was slaying went on and on and on.

I guess I wasn't too good at hiding what I thought because the little brown dude—name of Robin Goodfellow, but he tagged Puck—turned to me and asked what I thought. I could've lied, but he didn't look like he was having such a good time either, so I told him.

"Too bad you've got no decent tunes with you."

"I do." I tapped the player on my belt. "But I'd need a deck to plug in to."

"I could take care of that."

"Bonus!"

I handed over my player, and next thing I knew, The Bedrockers were blasting out at a hundred and twenty decibels.

The queen, *my* queen, whirled around so fast it was all hair and drapery stuff for a minute. Once that settled and I got a look at her face, there was, like, a second where she looked totally scary. Then Puck told her it was my sound, and she chilled, although her smile seemed a little forced.

I spent a couple of songs teaching the crowd to move, and I gotta hand it to them, for all they looked like they had a collective stick up their butts, they sure could dance.

Worn out by the exertions I would not dignify in calling dance, Tommy Lane spent the night asleep, so I did not even gain the small physical pleasure I might have from his presence. When he woke, he was annoyingly insistent upon eating and would not travel until he had broken his fast. Barely concealing my impatience, I had the sprites bring him bread and honey and clear water, as much as at this time I would have preferred him to have been fed with insects and the dregs of a swamp. Or better still, fed to insects and lost within the swamp.

Although Puck had returned to my husband's Court, I did not trust his absence and resolved to keep up the pretence until the boy was gone.

With no intention of travelling to the crossing at a mortal's pace, I took his hand and we were there. Unfortunately, we were not alone.

"Sending him back so soon, Majesty?"

"Why should I not? I have wrung from him all his strength."

At that moment, the boy chose to fling himself down a sheer rock face then up and over a bank of earth. Folding himself near in two, he clutched at his board, spun about in the air, and landed with a merry whoop.

"Seems to have gotten his strength back. Your husband,

my lord Oberon, is pleased you have found amusement. How unfortunate that you find he does not suit."

I could well read the implication between his words. As much as accuse me of a foolish choice. I would not have that. Much angered, my voice sheathed in ice, I said, "Then my husband, the Lord Oberon, will be pleased to hear that I am not sending him back, but rather gifting him with passage between our worlds, so that he might amuse himself as he will." Masking my fury, I called Tommy Lane to my side and opened the way. "You may go once each day to the place that I found you."

"You trying to get rid of me?"

From his smile I could see that he was making fun, and for the sake of our audience, I denied it.

"Her Majesty grants you a great gift," my husband's irritating emissary declared. "Do you not, Majesty?"

"Yes," I snapped before I thought.

A Faerie gift, once given, can not be recalled.

In order for me now to be rid of Tommy Lane, the decision to leave must be his.

I had it all. A major babe, servants, and great food—after a few tries, they even managed a decent burger and fries—I could ride when I wanted, and some of the fairy dudes were starting to catch on.

"Finvarra, what are you doing?"

He dropped to one knee, his waist-length hair wrapping

around him like a silken curtain. "I believe it is called a nollie, Majesty. In essence, an ollie performed by tapping the nose of the board instead of the tail."

My lip curled, almost of its own volition, and my hand rose to teach him such a lesson as would last the length of an immortal life. Unfortunately, at that moment Tommy Lane dropped down out of the trees, followed by that nuisance Puck.

"Hey Finvar! Rad move!"

"Your boy's really livening up the place," Puck announced, leaping off a board of his own. With no iron on the original, Faerie magic had been able to duplicate it easily. No one knew exactly what aluminium was, except that it wasn't iron. "Isn't it great?"

All three waited for my answer.

I locked my temper behind an indulgent smile. "It is."

Tommy Lane waved up toward the line of bark ripped in looping patterns from the inter-locking branches of the trees. "Did you know that Disney used boards to work out how Tarzan would move?"

"No."

It seemed my husband had not yet tired of the bothersome Puck's reports.

I would have to get creative.

Riding the trees was fine, but it was hard to keep it real; there were just some moves I couldn't do on bark, no matter how broad the branch. And sometimes I rolled right through living space, and that was just whack. Also more danger than I needed in my life; some of those dudes had really big swords. So, every day, I went back to the skate park.

I didn't see the girl at first; I saw the flowers. Three big, pink roses sprayed onto the side of the pipe. She wasn't easy to spot because she was kneeling down at the bottom of the third rose, painting in her tag. Her green jacket kind of blended in with all the foliage.

I mounted up and carved my way down to the bottom just as she stood. Her tag read Janet. Given that she was at the bottom of the pipe and couldn't get away, she stood her ground.

"Nice work," I said. "I haven't seen you around here before."

"My old man doesn't want me coming here. Says I'll meet the wrong sort." She shrugged. "I come anyway. I've seen you."

"You have?"

"Duh, you haunt this place. Yesterday afternoon, I saw that super high switch heelflip you did."

"Actually, it was switch front heelflip, switch heelflip, backside tailslide and a fakie hardflip."

"Wow."

"Yeah." It was good to talk to someone who understood. She was riding an urban assault board, way bigger than most girls like at forty inches, and I could see her eyeing my pro model. I have no idea what made me say it, but I stepped off and pushed my board over. "Go on. You know you want to."

Her eyes widened. Letting someone else on your ride was more intimate than screwing, and I could tell from her expression, she'd never done this before. Finally, she nodded and pushed her ride toward me. "What the hell. The front trucks are a little tight."

She was right and I bailed coming out of a tailslide, trying to carve left across the bowl. Took most of the landing on my right shoulder, but still buffed a strip of skin off my jaw. Late afternoon, she came off some air and into a fakie, shifted her weight wrong, hit, and rolled up, blood seeping through the knee of her cargos.

Bonded in blood. Cool.

With her leg locked up, she was done for the day. Using her board like a crutch, she hobbled to the edge of the park and turned to stare back at me. "You want to go get some fries or something?"

Actually I did, but Annie was expecting me back, and...

Janet snorted. "You got a girl. I should've known."

While I was thinking of something, anything, to say, she limped away.

❉

He was bleeding when he returned to me that night, and he stank of mortal company. I would have demanded to know her name, but that vexatious Puck lingered still about, and I would not have him carry tales of a mortal lover who dared to cheat on me.

Later, with the nettlesome sprite safely in sight, but out of earshot as he sought to annoy me by having Tommy Lane teach him new tricks, I got the whole story from the Loireag.

A girl.

I would use her.

That night, as he slept, I cloaked myself in shadow and did what I had not done for many long years—I walked amid the mortal race. The girl was easy enough to find; her blood had mixed with his, and his was mine.

She sat by the entrance to her dwelling. Within, raised voices discussed locking her in her room until she told them the name of the boy she was seeing.

In guise of one Tommy Lane would believe, wearing the face of my husband's emissary—which had, of late, become as familiar to me as my own—I sat down beside her. "They sound angry."

"Who the hell are you?"

Of old, the young were much politer. "I bring you word from Tommy Lane."

"Who?"

Thus I discovered the reason she had not told her elders the name of the boy. "You met him today at the ring of stone by Carterhaugh Pond. You rode his board and he yours."

"Yeah, so?"

"He is in grave danger. Tomorrow night, the Queen of Faerie will take his life."

"Where?"

I sighed. "She will end his life."

"Why?"

"Because a tithe to darkness must be paid, and she will not sacrifice an immortal knight when a mortal man is close at hand."

"Look, I don't know what you're on, but I got troubles of my own, so make like a leaf and get lost."

I drew her gaze around to mine, captured it, and held it. "Do you believe me now?" I demanded when, after many heartbeats, I released her.

She drew in a long, shuddering breath. "I guess."

As that appeared to be as good as I would get, I continued. "You must go to the park as the sun leaves the sky, and when the Queen arrives to claim him, you must snatch him from his board and hold him tight." A possible problem occurred to me. "Are you afraid of snakes?"

"No."

"Good. Do not fear although he be turned within your grasp into angry beasts or red-hot iron or burning lead or…"

"Does this fairy tale have a point? Because if I'm not inside in five minutes my old man's going to come out here and kick my ass."

"If you hold tightly to young Tommy Lane, he will in time become himself again. Then you must wrap him in your mantle green."

"My what?"

I sighed again. "Wrap him in your green jacket, and the spell will be broken."

Annie looked real pleased with herself the next morning, and when I went for a quickie before breakfast, she was so into it, it was kind of scary. I mean, I liked her enthusiasm, but man…

She stretched out on the bed looking all catlike and said, "Wait at the park this evening until I come for you. I have a surprise planned."

Later, everyone I passed on the way to the park said good-bye.

I was making my third run down over Janet's roses, when

it was like she suddenly appeared. I looked up on the lip, and there she was.

I flipped up beside her. She looked pissed.

"Are you real or what?"

"What?"

"Bastard!" She punched me in the arm.

"What are you talking about?"

And then she told me this bullshit story some short brown dude told her about my Annie and sacrificing me tonight and crap.

"It's a Halloween prank," I told her.

She snorted. "I thought so. The whole thing's a friggin' lie!"

"Not all of it," I admitted. I told her my side of the story, and she snorted again.

"Jeez, you are so lame! If that's true, then what makes the story I got told not true? It sounds to me like the Queen wants more than your bod. You said she looked pleased with herself. She said she has a surprise planned. Everyone said goodbye to you when you left. Duh! How many times have you bailed on your head?"

When Janet put it that way, it all began to make a horrible amount of sense. Puck. The short brown dude had to have been Puck. He liked me, and he didn't seem to like my Annie much. I guess now I knew why.

I stepped onto my board. "I'm so out of here."

And that was my cue. I could not allow him to merely ride away; the power of the gift I'd given him had to be broken or I would ever live with the nagging feeling that someday he might return.

As I stepped into the mortal world, I was pleased to see the girl wrap her arms around young Tommy Lane and drag him off his board. I wrapped myself in terrible beauty and, as she tried to stare me down, raised a hand.

First I turned him to an adder, and Janet held him close, although her language would have withered apples on the tree.

Then I turned him to a lion wild, and Janet released one hand and smacked the beast upon the nose.

Then I turned him to a red hot bar of iron, and Janet screamed and threw him in the pond, throwing her smouldering jacket in after him.

Close enough.

Another wailing visit from the Loireag was little enough price to pay.

As I removed the glamour and he was once again Tommy Lane, I cried out, "If I had known some lady'd borrowed thee, I would have plucked out your eyes and put in eyes of tree. And had I known of this before I came from home, I would have plucked out your heart and put in a heart of stone!"

"Possessive much?" Janet snarled from the edge of the pond.

Dragging Janet's jacket behind him, Tommy Lane waded to the shore, shaking his head. "Babe, we are *so* over."

I had thought that was the point I was making.

When I stepped back into Faerie, it was to find Robin Goodfellow awaiting me.

"Ah yes, the old held by mortal maid shtick." He scratched reflectively beneath one arm. "Funny thing, though, I could've sworn that tithe went out after seven years, not seven days."

Had it only been seven days? It had seemed so very much longer. "Shut up," I told him.

"Hey, rules were followed, traditions upheld, I got nothing to say." He bowed, sweeping an imaginary hat against the ground. "If Your Majesty has no further need of me."

I forbore to remind him that I never *had* need of him nor ever would. He waved in his most irritatingly jaunty manner and sped through the deepening twilight toward the Lord Oberon's Court, indulging in a series of kickflips as he rode out of sight.

A velvet hush settled over my Court as, with stately grace, I moved among my knights and ladies. As I settled upon a grassy bank and allowed my ladies to twine starflowers in the midnight fall of my hair, I came to an inescapable conclusion.

It was entirely possible that I had remarkably bad taste in men.

This story was originally published in 1992. Twenty-two years ago. I honestly have no idea where the idea came from or why I made the choices I made when writing it. Seriously, twenty-two years. I don't always remember what I did last Tuesday. "Write something for a Christmas anthology," I was asked. "Okay," I said. And I'm paraphrasing, because I don't remember the conversation either.

I will say that the old farmhouse in the story belonged to my great-grandparents and it cost a fortune in oil to heat, so the only really warm room in the house was the kitchen where the wood-stove reigned. No one in my immediate family ever kept pigs in the porch.

I also remember that I showed an early draft of this story to Michelle Sagara when we were working together at Bakka Books in Toronto, and, because her brain doesn't default to sexy times, she had a completely different idea of what the music was offering. For Michelle's sake, I made it more obvious in later drafts.

I'LL BE HOME
FOR CHRISTMAS

Yes, you'll be dressed in holiday style if you come down to Big Bob's pre-Christmas clothing sale. All the fashions, all the frills, all major credit cards accepted..."

"Are we there yet?"

"Soon, honey."

"How soon?"

"Soon."

"I'm gonna be sick."

Elaine Montgomery took her eyes off the road just long enough to shoot a panicked glance at her daughter's flushed face. "We're almost there, Katie. Can't you hold on just a little bit longer?"

"No!" The last letter stretched and lengthened into a wail that completely drowned out the tinny sound of the car radio and threatened to shatter glass.

As Elaine swerved the car toward the shoulder, an echo-

ing wail rose up from the depths of the beige plastic cat carrier securely strapped down in the back seat. The last time
she'd assumed Katie could hold on for the two kilometres to
the next rest stop, it had taken her over an hour to clean the
car—which had allowed the cat's tranquilizers to wear off long
before they arrived at their destination.

Neither Katie nor the cat were very good travellers.

"Mommy!"

Wet gravel spun under the tires as she fought the car and
trailer to a standstill. "Just another second, honey. Grit your
teeth." *How many times can you throw up one lousy cheese sandwich?*
she wondered, unbuckling her seatbelt and reaching for her
daughter's. *Thank God she's not still in the kiddie carseat.* It had
taken a good twenty minutes and an advanced engineering
degree to get Katie in and out of the safety seat, and, here
and now, all signs indicated she had closer to twenty seconds.

"It's all right, baby. Mommy's got you." She slid them both
out the passenger door and went to her knees in a puddle to
better steady the four-year-old's shaking body. December rain
drove icy fingers down the back of her neck, and not for the
first time since leaving Toronto that morning, Elaine wondered what the hell she was doing heading into the middle of
nowhere two weeks before Christmas with a four-year-old, a
very pissed off cat, and all her worldly goods.

Trying to survive, came the answer.

I knew that. She sighed and kissed Katie's wet curls.

"Ms. Montgomery?" Upon receiving an affirmative answer,
the woman who'd come out of the house as the car pulled up

popped open an umbrella and hurried forward. "I'm Catherine Henderson. Your late aunt's lawyer? So nice to finally meet you at last. I was afraid you weren't going to make it before I had to leave. Here, let me take the cat..."

Elaine willingly surrendered the cat-carrier, tucked Katie up under one arm, and grabbed for their bag of essentials with the other. The two-story brick farmhouse loomed up out of the darkness like the haven she hoped it was, and feeling more than just a little numb, she followed the steady stream of chatter up onto the porch and into the kitchen.

"No need to lock the car, you're miles away from anyone who might want to steal it out here. I hope you don't mind going around to the back, I can't remember the last time the front door was opened. Careful on that step, there's a crack in the cement. The porch was a later addition to the original farmhouse, which was built by your late aunt's father in the twenties. You'll have to excuse the smell; your aunt got a bit, well, eccentric later in life and kept a pair of pigs in here over last winter. I had the place scoured and disinfected after we spoke on the phone, but I'm afraid the smell is going to be with you for a while." She dropped the umbrella into a pail by the door and heaved the carrier up onto the kitchen table. "Good heavens, he's a big one isn't he? Did he wail like that all the way from Toronto?"

"No." Elaine put Katie down and brushed wet hair back off her face. "Only for the last hundred kilometres or so."

"I'll let him out, Mommy." Small fingers struggled with the latch for a second, then a grey and white blur leapt from the table and disappeared under the tattered lounge by the window.

"Leave him be, Katie." A quick grab kept her daughter from burrowing beneath the furniture with the cat. "He needs to be alone for a while."

"Okay." Katie turned, looked speculatively up at the lawyer and announced, "I puked all over the car."

"I'm sorry to hear that." Catherine took the pronouncement in stride. "If you're feeling sick again," she crossed the kitchen and opened one of four identical doors, "the bathroom is through here." Reaching for the next door over, she continued. "This is the bedroom your aunt used—I suggest you use it as well as it's the only room in the house that's insulated. This is the hall, leading to the front door and the stairs—another four bedrooms up there, but as I said, uninsulated. And this is the cellar."

Elaine took an almost involuntary step forward. "What was that?"

"What was what?" the other woman asked carefully, closing the cellar door.

"The music. I heard music... just for a second. It sounded like, like..." Obviously, the lawyer hadn't heard it, so Elaine let the explanation trail off.

"Yes, well, these old houses make a lot of strange noises. There's an oil furnace down there, but it must be close to thirty-five years old, so I wouldn't count on it too much. I think your aunt depended on the woodstove. You do know how to use a woodstove, don't you?"

"I think I can figure it out." The question had hovered just on the edge of patronizing, and Elaine decided not to admit her total lack of experience. *You burn wood; how hard could it be? Whole forests burn down on their own every year.*

"Good. I've left a casserole and a litre of milk in the fridge. I don't imagine you'll want to cook after that long drive. You've got my number; if you need anything, don't hesitate to call."

"Thank you." As Catherine retrieved her umbrella, Elaine held open the porch door and wrinkled her nose. "Um, I was wondering, what happened to the pigs when my aunt died?"

"Worried about wild boars tearing up the property? You needn't; the pigs shuffled off this mortal coil months before your aunt did. There might still be packages marked Porky or Petunia in the freezer out in the woodshed."

Elaine closed the door on Catherine's laugh and leaned for a moment against the peeling paint. Porky and Petunia. Right. It had been a very long day. She started as skinny arms wrapped around her leg.

"Mommy? I'm hungry."

"I'm not surprised." She took a deep breath, turned, and scooped her daughter up onto her hip. "But first we're both putting on some dry clothes. How does that sound?"

Katie shrugged. "Sounds okay."

On the way to the bedroom, Elaine dropped the overnight case and pulled the cellar door open a crack, just to check. There was a faint, liquid trill of sound, and then the only thing she could hear was water running into the cistern.

"Mommy?"

"Did you hear the music, Katie?"

Katie listened with all the intensity only a small child could muster. "No," she said at last. "No music. What did it sound like?"

"Nothing honey. Mommy must have been imagining it." It had sounded like an invitation, but not the kind that could be discussed with a four-year-old. It probably should have been frightening, but it wasn't. Each note had sent shivers of anticipation dancing over her skin. Elaine was willing to bet the farm—well, maybe not that, as this rundown old place was the only refuge they had—that she hadn't been imagining anything.

The forest was the most alive place she'd ever been; lush and tangled, with bushes reaching up, and trees reaching down, and wild flowers and ferns tucked in every possible nook and cranny. She danced through it to the wild call of the music and when she realized she was naked, it didn't seem to matter. Nothing scratched, nothing prickled, and the ground under her bare feet had the resilience of a good foam mattress.

Oh, yes! the music agreed.

The path the music lead her down had been danced on before. Her steps followed the imprint of a pair of cloven hooves.

She could see a clearing up ahead, a figure outlined in the brilliant sunlight, pan pipes raised to lips, an unmistakable silhouette, intentions obvious. She felt her cheeks grow hot.

What am I thinking of? Her feet lost a step in the dance. *I'm responsible for a four- year-old child. I can't just go running off to... to... well, I can't just go running off.*

Why not? the music asked indignantly.

"Because I can't! Yi!" She teetered, nearly fell, and made a sudden grab for the door frame. The cellar stairs fell away, dark and steep, and from somewhere down below the music made one final plea. It wailed its disappointment as she slammed the cellar door closed.

A little dreaming, a little sleepwalking, a little... Well, never mind. Elaine shoved a chair up under the doorknob and tried not to run back to the bedroom she was sharing with Katie. *I'm just reacting to the first night in a new house. Nothing strange about that... And old furnaces make a lot of... noises.*

Of course, she had to admit as she scrambled under the covers and snuggled up against the warmth of her sleeping daughter, old furnaces didn't usually make lecherous suggestions.

"How much!?"

The oil man wiped his hands on a none-too-clean rag. "You got a 200 gallon tank there, Ms. Montgomery. Oil's thirty-six point two cents a litre, there's a about four and a half litres a gallon, that's, uh..." His brow furrowed as he worked out the math. "Three hundred and twenty-five dollars and eighty cents, plus G.S.T."

Elaine set the grubby piece of paper down on the kitchen table and murmured, "Just like it says on the bill."

He beamed. "That's right."

She had just over five hundred dollars in the account she'd transferred to the local bank. Enough, she'd thought, given that they no longer needed to pay rent, to give her and Katie a couple of months to get settled before she had to find work. Apparently, she'd thought wrong. "I'll get my cheque book." If her aunt kept the house warm with the woodstove, she must've been re-lighting the fire every half an hour. Which was about as long as Elaine had been able to get it to burn.

The oil man watched as she wrote out his cheque, then scrawled paid in full across the bill and handed it to her with a flourish. "Don't you worry," he said as she winced. "Your late aunt managed to get by spendin' only twelve hundred dollars for heatin' last winter."

"Only twelve hundred dollars," Elaine repeated weakly.

"That's right." He paused in the door and grinned back at her. "'Course, not to speak ill of the dead, but I think she had other ways of keepin' warm."

"What do you mean?" At this point any other way sounded better than twelve hundred dollars.

"Well, one time, about, oh, four, five years ago now, I showed up a little earlier than I'd said, and I saw her comin' up out of the basement with the strangest sort of expression on her face. Walkin' a bit funny too. I think," he leaned forward and nodded sagely, "I think she was down there having a bit of a nip."

Elaine blinked. "But she never drank."

The oil man tapped his nose. "That's what they say. Anyway, Merry Christmas, Ms. Montgomery. I'll see you in the new year."

"Yes, Merry Christmas." She watched the huge truck roar away. "Three hundred and twenty-five dollars and eighty cents plus G.S.T. merrier for you anyway..."

"Mommy!"

The wail of a four-year-old in distress lifted every hair on her head and had her moving before her conscious mind even registered the direction of the cry. She charged out the back door without bothering to put on a coat, raced around the corner of the building, and almost tripped over the kneeling figure of her daughter.

"What is it, Katie? Are you hurt?"

Katie lifted a tear-streaked face, and Elaine got a glimpse of the bloody bundle in her lap. "Sid-cat's been killeded!"

❈

"Ms. Montgomery?"

Elaine moved Katie's head off her lap and stood to face the vet, leaving the sleeping child sprawled across three of the waiting-room chairs. There'd been a lot of blood staining the white expanse of his ruff, but Sid-cat had not actually been dead—although his life had been in danger a number of times during the wild drive in to the vet's. There are some things Fords are not meant to do on icy, back-country roads.

Dr. Levin brushed a strand of long, dark hair back off her face and smiled reassuringly. "He's going to be all right. I think we've even managed to save the eye."

"Thank God." She hadn't realized she'd been holding her breath until she let it out. "Do you know what attacked him?"

The vet nodded. "Another cat."

"Are you sure?"

"No doubt about it. He did a little damage himself, and the fur caught in his claws was definitely cat. You've moved into your aunt's old place, haven't you?"

"Yes..."

"Well, I wouldn't doubt there's a couple of feral cats living in what's left of that old barn of hers. You're isolated enough out there that they've probably interbred into vicious, brainless animals." She frowned. "Now, I don't hold with this as a rule, but housecats like Sid don't stand a chance against feral cats, and you've got a child to think of. You should consider hiring someone to clear them out."

"I'll think about it."

"Good." Dr. Levin smiled again. "Sid'll have to stay here for a few days, of course. Let's see, it's December 20th today, call me on the 24th. I think we can have him home for Christmas."

❄

When they got back to the farmhouse, a line of paw prints marked the fresh snow up to the porch door and away. In spite of the bitter cold, they could smell the reason for the visit as soon as they reached the steps.

"Boy pee!" Katie pronounced disdainfully, rubbing a mittened hand over her nose.

Every entrance to the house had been similarly marked.

The house itself was freezing. The woodstove had gone out. The furnace appeared to be having no effect.

Elaine looked down at her shivering daughter and seriously considered shoving her back into the car, cramming everything she could into the trunk, and heading back to the city. *At least in the city, I know what's going on.* She sagged against the cellar door and rubbed her hand across her eyes as a hopeful series of notes rose up from below. *At least in the city, I wasn't hearing things.* But they didn't have a life in the city anymore.

Come and play, said the music. *Come and...*

I can't! she told it silently. *Shut up!*

"Mommy? Are you okay?"

With an effort, she shook herself free. "I'm fine Katie. Mommy's just worried about Sid-cat."

Katie nodded solemnly. "Me too."

"I know what we should do, baby. Let's put up the Christmas tree." Elaine forced a smile and hoped it didn't look as false as it felt. "Here it is December 20th and we haven't even started getting ready for Christmas."

"We go to the woods and chop it down?" Katie grabbed at her mother's hand. "There's an axe in the shed."

"No, sweetheart. Mommy isn't much good with an axe." Chopping wood for the stove had been a nightmare. "We'll use the old tree this year."

"Okay." The artificial tree and the box marked decorations had been left by the dining room table. Katie raced towards them, stopped, and looked back at her mother, her face squeezed into a worried frown. "Will Santa be able to find me way out here? Does he know where we went?"

Elaine reached down and laid a hand lightly on Katie's curls. "Santa can find you anywhere," she promised. Katie's presents had been bought with the last of her severance pay, the day she got the call that her aunt had left her the family farm. No matter what, Katie was getting a Christmas.

The six-foot, fake spruce seemed dwarfed by the fifteen-foot ceilings in the living room and even the decorations didn't do much to liven it up, although Katie very carefully hung two boxes of tinsel over the lower four feet.

"It needs the angel," she said, stepping back and critically surveying her handiwork. "Put the angel on now, Mommy."

"Well, it certainly needs something," Elaine agreed, mirroring her daughter's expression. Together, very solemnly, they lifted the angel's case out of the bottom of the box.

Carefully, Elaine undid the string that held the lid secure.

"Tell me the angel story again, Mommy."

"The angel was a present," Elaine began, shifting so that Katie's warm weight slid under her arm and up against her heart, "from my father to my mother on the day I was born."

"So she's really old."

"Not so very old!" The protest brought a storm of giggles. "He told my mother that, as she'd given him an angel..."

"That was you."

"...that he'd give her one. And every Christmas he'd sit the angel on the very top of the Christmas tree, and she'd glow." When Elaine had been small, she'd thought the angel glowed on her own and had been more than a little disappointed to discover the tiny light tucked back in-between her wings. "When you were born, my parents..."

"Grandma and Grandpa."

"That's right, Grandma and Grandpa..." Who had known their granddaughter for only a year before the car crash. "... gave the angel to me because I'd given them another angel."

"Me," Katie finished triumphantly.

"You," Elaine agreed, kissed the top of Katie's head and folded back the tissue paper. She blew on her fingers to warm them then slid her hand very gently under the porcelain body and lifted the angel out of the box. The head wobbled once, then fell to the floor and shattered into a hundred pieces.

Elaine looked down at the shards of porcelain, at the tangled ruin of golden-white hair lying in their midst, and burst into tears.

❄

Come and play! called the music. *Be happy! Come and...*

"No!"

"No what, Mommy?"

"Never mind, pet. Go back to sleep."

"Did you have a bad dream?"

"Yes." Except it had been a very good dream.

"Don't worry, Mommy. Santa will bring another angel. I asked him to."

Elaine gently touched Katie's cheek then swiped at her own. *Isn't it enough we're stuck in this freezing cold house*—only the bedroom was tolerable—*in the middle of nowhere with no money? I thought we could make this a home. I thought I could give her a Christmas at least...*

But when the angel had shattered, Christmas had shattered with it.

"I'm tired of eating pigs."

"I know, baby, so am I." Porky and Petunia had become the main course of almost every meal they'd eaten since they arrived. Elaine had thought, had hoped they could have a turkey for Christmas, but with the size of the oil bill—not to mention oil bills yet to come—added to the cost of keeping the cat at the vet for four days, it looked like a turkey was out of the question.

"I don't want pigs anymore!"

"There isn't anything else."

Katie pushed out her lower lip and pushed the pieces of chop around on her plate.

Elaine sighed. There were only so many ways to prepare...

pigs, and she had run out of new ideas. Her aunt's old cook-books had been less than no help. They were so old that recipes called for a penny-weight of raisins and began the instructions for roasting a chicken with a nauseatingly detailed lesson on how to pluck and gut it.

❆

"Mommy. Mommy, wake up!"

"What is it, Katie?"

"Mommy, tomorrow is Christmas!"

Elaine just barely stopped herself from saying, *So what?*

"And today we bring Sid-cat home!"

And today we pay Sid-cat's vet bill. She didn't know what she was looking forward to less, a cold Christmas spent with Porky and Petunia or the emptying out of her chequing account.

Bundling a heavy wool sweater on over her pyjamas, she went out to see if the fire in the woodstove had survived the night and if maybe a cup of coffee would be possible before noon.

Not, she thought as a draft of cold air swirled around her legs through the open bedroom door, *that I have very high hopes.*

"Katie!" A layer of ash laid a grey patina over everything within a three foot radius of the stove. "Did you do this?"

A small body pushed between her and the counter. "You said, stay away from the stove." Katie swung her teddy bear by one leg, the arc of its head drawing a thick, fuzzy line through the ash on the floor. "So, I stayed away. Honest truly."

"Then how...?"

Teddy drew another arc. "The wind came down the chimney whoosh?"

"Maybe. Maybe it was the wind." But Elaine didn't really

believe that. Just like she didn't really believe she saw a tiny, slippered footprint right at the point where a tiny person would have to brace their weight to empty the ash pan. Heart in her throat, she stepped forward, squatted, and swiped at the print with the edge of her sweater. She didn't believe in it. It didn't exist.

The sudden crash of breaking glass, however, couldn't be ignored.

Slowly, she turned and faced the cellar door.

"That came from downstairs," Katie said helpfully, brushing ash off her teddy bear's head onto her pyjamas.

"I know that, Katie. Mommy has ears. Go sit in the chair by the window." She looked down at her daughter's trembling lip and added a terse, "Please."

Dragging her feet, Katie went to the chair.

"Now stay there. Mommy's going down to the cellar to see what broke the window." *Mommy's out of her mind...*

"I want to go too!"

"Stay there! Please. It's probably just some animal trying to get in out of the cold." The cellar door opened without the expected ominous creak, and, although Elaine would have bet money against it, a flick of the switch flooded as much of the cellar as she could see with light. *Of course, there's always the part I can't see.*

The temperature dropped as she moved down the stairs, and she shivered as she crossed the second step; until this moment, the furthest she'd descended. At the bottom of the stairs, she could see the cistern, the furnace, wheezing away in its corner, and the rusted bulk of the oil tank. An icy breeze against her right cheek pulled her around.

Probably just some animal trying to get in out of the cold, she repeated, taking one step, two, three. *A lot it knows...* By the fourth step she'd drawn even with the window and was squinting in the glare of morning sun on snow. *Oh, my God.* The glass had been forced out, not in, and the tracks leading away were three-pronged and deep. She whirled around, caught sight of a flash of colour, and froze.

The feather was about six inches long and brilliantly banded with red and gold. She bent to pick it up and caught sight of another, a little smaller and a little mashed. The second feather lay half in shadow at the base of the rough stone wall. The third, fourth and fifth feathers were caught on the stone at the edge of a triangular hole the size of Elaine's head.

Something had forced its way out of that hole and then out of the cellar.

Barely breathing, Elaine backed up a step, the feather falling from suddenly nerveless fingers.

"Mommy?"

She didn't remember getting to the top of the cellar stairs. "Get dressed, Katie." With an effort, she kept her voice steady. "We're going in to get Sid." *And we're going to keep driving. And we're not going to stop until Easter.*

"...I don't expect anyone to have that kind of cash right at Christmas." Dr. Levin smiled down at Katie, who had her face pressed up against the bars of the cat carrier. "I'll send you a bill in the new year and we can work out a payment schedule."

"You're sure?" Elaine asked incredulously.

"I'm very sure."

The vet in Toronto had accepted credit cards, but certainly not credit. Under the circumstances, it seemed ungracious to suggest that they might not be around in the new year. Elaine swallowed once and squared her shoulders. "Dr. Levin, did you know my aunt?"

"Not well, but I knew her."

"Did she ever mention anything strange going on in that house?"

Ebony eyebrows rose. "What do you mean, strange?"

Elaine waved her hands helplessly, searching for the words. "You know, strange."

The vet laughed. "Well, as I said, we weren't close. The only thing I can remember her saying about the house is that she could never live anywhere else. Why? Have strange things been happening?"

"You might say that..."

"Give it a little while," Dr. Levin advised sympathetically. "You're not used to country life."

"True..." Elaine admitted slowly. *Was that it?*

"If it helps, I know your aunt was happy out there. She always smiled like she had a wonderful secret. I often envied her that smile."

Elaine, scrabbling in the bottom of her purse for a pencil, barely heard her. Maybe she just wasn't used to living in the country. Maybe that was all it was. "One more thing, if you don't mind, Doctor." She turned over the cheque she hadn't needed to fill out and quickly sketched the pattern of tracks that had lead away from the basement window. "Can you tell me what kind of an animal would make these?"

Dr. Levin pursed her lips and studied the slightly wobbly

lines. "It's a type of bird, that's for certain. Although I wouldn't like to commit myself one hundred percent, I'd say it's a chicken."

Elaine blinked. "A chicken?"

"That's right." She laughed. "Don't tell me you've got a feral chicken out there as well as a feral cat?"

Elaine managed a shaky laugh in return. "Seems like."

"Well, keep Sid inside, make sure you give him the antibiotics, call me if he shows any sign of pain, and..." She reached into the pocket of her lab coat and pulled out a pair of candy canes. "...have a merry Christmas."

"Mommy?" Katie poked one finger into her mother's side. "Sid-cat doesn't like the car. Let's go home."

Elaine bit her lip. Home. Well, they couldn't sit in the parking lot forever. Dr. Levin had said it was a chicken. Who could be afraid of a chicken? It had probably been living down in the basement for some time. It had finally run out of food, so it had left. There was probably nothing behind that hole in the wall but a bit of loose earth.

Her aunt had never said there was anything strange about the house and she'd lived there all her adult life. Had been happy there.

Where else did they have to go?

The fire in the woodstove was still burning when they got home. Elaine stared down at it in weary astonishment and hastily shoved another piece of wood in before it should change its mind and go out. The kitchen was almost warm.

Very carefully, she pulled Sid-cat out of the carrier and settled him in a shallow box lined with one of Katie's outgrown sweaters. He stared up at her with his one good eye, blinked, yawned, gave just enough of a purr so as not to seem ungracious, and went back to sleep.

Katie looked from the cat to her half-eaten candy cane to her mother. "Tomorrow is Christmas," she said solemnly. "It doesn't feel like Christmas."

"Oh, Katie..."

Leaving her daughter squatting by the box, "standing guard in case that federal cat comes back", Elaine went into the living room and stared at the Christmas tree. If only the angel hadn't broken. She thought she could cope with everything else, could pull a sort of Christmas out of the ruins, if only the angel still looked down from the top of the tree.

Maybe she could glue it back together.

The ruins lay on the dining room table, covered with an ancient linen napkin. A tiny corpse in a country morgue...

That's certainly the Christmas spirit, Elaine... She bit her lip and flicked the napkin back. One bright green glass eye stared up at her from its nest of shattered porcelain. *Oh God...*

"MOMMY!"

She was moving before the command had time to get from brain to feet.

"MOM-MEEEE!"

Katie was backed into a corner of the kitchen, one arm up over her face, the other waving around trying to drive off a flock of...

Of pixies?

They were humanoid, sexless, about eight inches tall with a double pair of gossamer wings, and they glowed in all the colours of the rainbow. Long hair, the same iridescent shade as their skin, streamed around them, moving with an almost independent life of its own. Even from a distance they were beautiful, but as Elaine crossed the kitchen, she saw that her daughter's arms were bleeding from a number of nasty-looking scratches and a half a dozen of them had a hold of Katie's curls.

"Get away from her!" Elaine charged past the kitchen table, grabbed a magazine, rolled it on the run, and began flailing at the tiny bodies. She pulled a pink pixie off Katie's head and threw it across the kitchen. "Go back where you came from you, you overgrown bug!" It hit the wall beside the fridge, shook itself, buzzed angrily, and sped back to Katie.

"Mom-meee!"

"Keep your eyes covered, honey!" They swarmed so thick around the little girl that every swing knocked a couple out of the air. Unfortunately, it didn't seem to discourage them, although they did, finally, acknowledge the threat.

"Be careful, Mommy!" Katie wailed as the entire flock turned. "They bite!"

Their teeth weren't very big, but they were sharp.

The battle raged around the kitchen. Elaine soon bled from a number of small wounds. The pixies appeared to be no worse off than when they'd started even though they'd each been hit at least once.

A gold pixie perched for a moment on the table and hissed up at her, gnashing blood-stained teeth. Without thinking, Elaine slammed her aunt's old aluminium colander over it.

It shrank back from the sides and began hissing in earnest.

One down... The kitchen counter hit her in the small of the back. Elaine smashed her wrist against the cupboard, dislodging a purple pixie that had been attempting to chew her hand off, and groped around for a weapon. Dish rack, spatula, dish soap, spray can of snow...

Katie had wanted to write Merry Christmas on the kitchen window. They hadn't quite gotten around to it.

Elaine's fingers closed around the can. Knocking the lid off against the side of the sink, she nailed a lavender pixie at point-blank range.

The goopy white spray coated its wings, and it plummeted to the floor, hissing with rage.

"HA! I've got you now, you little... Take that! And that!"

The kitchen filled with the drifting clouds of a chemical blizzard.

"Mommy! They're leaving!"

Although a number of them were running rather than flying, the entire swarm appeared to be racing for the cellar door. With adrenaline sizzling along every nerve, Elaine followed. They weren't getting away from her that easily. She reached the bottom of the stairs in time to see the first of the pixies dive through the hole. Running full out, she managed to get in another shot at the half-dozen on foot before they disappeared and then, dropping to her knees, emptied the can after them.

"And may all your Christmases be white!" she screamed, sat back on her heels, and panted, feeling strong and triumphant and, for the first time in a long time, capable. She grinned down at the picture of Santa on the can. "I guess we showed them, didn't we?" Patting him on the cheek, she set the empty container down, noted it was a good thing she'd gotten the large, economy size, and turned her attention to the hole. The rock that had fallen out—or been pushed out—wasn't that large and could easily be manoeuvred back into place. She'd come down later with a can of mortar. Bucket of mortar? Someone at the hardware store would know.

Now that she really took the time to look at it, the hole actually occupied the lower corner of a larger patch in the wall. None of the stones were very big and although they'd been set carefully, they were obviously not part of the original construction. Squinting in the uncertain light, Elaine leaned forward and peered at a bit of red smeared across roughly the centre stone.

Was it blood?

It was Coral Dawn. She had a lipstick nearly the same shade in her purse. And the shape of the smear certainly suggested...

"Sealed with a kiss?"

Frowning, she poked at it with a fingertip.

The music crescendoed, and feelings not her own rode with it. Memories of... She felt herself flush. Sorrow at parting. Loneliness. Welcome. Annoyance that other, smaller creatures broke the rules and forced the passage.

Come and play! Come and...

A little stunned, Elaine lifted her finger. The music continued, but the feelings stopped. She swallowed and adjusted her jeans.

"I think she had other ways of keeping warm. Walkin' a bit funny too."

"She always smiled like she had a wonderful secret."

"A wonderful secret. Good lord." It was suddenly very warm in the cellar. If her aunt, her old, fragile aunt, who had obviously been a lot more flexible than she'd appeared, had accepted the music's invitation...

The scream of a furious cat jerked her head around and banished contemplation.

"Now what?" she demanded, scrambling to her feet and racing for the stairs. "Katie, did you let Sid-cat outside?"

"No." Katie met her at the cellar door, eyes wide. "It's two other cats. And a chicken."

Elaine gave her daughter a quick hug. "You stay here and guard Sid-cat. Mommy'll take care of it."

The pixie trapped under the colander hissed inarticulate threats.

"Shut up," she snapped without breaking stride. To her surprise, it obeyed. Grabbing her jacket, she headed out through the woodshed, snatching up the axe as she went. She didn't have a clue what she was going to do with it, but the weight felt good in her hand.

The cats were an identical muddy calico, thin with narrow heads, tattered ears, and vicious expressions. Bellies to the snow and ragged tails lashing from side to side, they were flanking the biggest chicken Elaine had ever seen. As she watched, one of the cats darted forward and the chicken lashed out with its tail.

Up until this moment, Elaine had never seen a chicken that hadn't been wrapped in cellophane, but even she knew that chickens did not have long, scaled, and, apparently, prehensile tails.

The first cat dodged the blow, while the second narrowly missed being eviscerated by a sideswipe from one of the bird's taloned feet. Elaine wasn't sure she should get involved, mostly because she wasn't sure whose side she should be on. Although the chicken *had* come from her cellar.

Growling low in its throat, the first cat attacked again, slid under a red and gold wing, and found itself face to face with its intended prey. To Elaine's surprise, the bird made no attempt to use its beak. It merely stared, unblinking, into the slitted yellow eyes of the cat.

The cat suddenly grew very still, its growl cut off in mid note, its tail frozen in mid lash.

All at once, choosing sides became very easy.

Still buzzing from her battle with the pixies, Elaine charged forward. The not-quite-a-chicken turned. Eyes squeezed shut, knuckles white around the haft, she swung the axe in a wild arc. Then again. And again.

The blade bit hard into something that resisted only briefly. Over the pounding of the blood in her ears, Elaine heard the sound of feathers beating against air and something stumbling in the snow. Something slammed against her shins. Opening her eyes a crack, she risked a look.

The headless body of the bird lay, not entirely still, at her feet. She leapt back as the tail twitched and nearly fell over the stone statue of the cat. Its companion glared at her, slunk in, grabbed the severed head, and, trailing blood from its prize, raced under a tangle of snow-laden bushes.

"I am not going to be sick," Elaine told herself sternly, leaning on the axe. Actually, the instruction appeared unnecessary. Although she was a little out of breath, she felt exalted rather than nauseous. She poked at the corpse with her foot. Whatever remaining life force had animated it after its head had been chopped off appeared to have ebbed.

"And it's really most sincerely dead," she muttered. "Now what?"

Then the crunch of small bones from the bushes gave her an idea, and she smiled.

Elaine watched Katie instructing Sid-cat in the use of her new paint box and decided that this could be one of the best Christmases she'd had in years. The woodstove seemed to be behaving, throwing out enough heat to keep the kitchen and the living room warm and cosy. She'd found a bag of frozen cranberries jammed under one of Porky's generous shoulders, and a pot of cranberry sauce now bubbled and steamed on top of the stove. Thanks to the instructions in her aunt's old cookbooks, the smell of roasting... well, the smell of roasting filled the house.

Her gaze drifted up to the top of the tree. Although the old angel had been an important part of her old life and she'd always feel its loss, the new angel was an equally important symbol of her fight to make a new life, and find a new home for herself and her daughter. Tethered with a bit of ribbon, its wings snow-covered in honour of the season, the pixie tossed glowing golden hair back off its face and gnawed on a bit of raw pork.

"Mommy?"

"Yes, Katie."

"Didn't Santa bring you any presents?"

"Mommy got her present early this morning. While you were still asleep."

"Did you like it?"

"Very, very much."

On the stereo, a Welsh choir sang Hosannas. Rising up from the cellar, wrapping around a choirboy's clear soprano, a set of pipes trilled out smug hosannas of their own.

A long, long time ago, I was a Brownie. In fact, I was a Brownie for two extra years. I started early because a new Brownie troop had just been formed and they needed girls, so my best friend and I were allowed in even though we were underage. I stayed late because the local Guide troop had no room, so the six of us ready to fly up were made junior leaders and allowed to pretty much run things for a year. Not surprisingly, after we finally did fly up and were suddenly low girl in the pecking order again, we all quit.

These days, the only interaction I have with Guiding is the same interaction everyone else in town has. During cookie season, a swarm of Sparks—very small girls in pink sweat-shirts—surrounds anyone who gets out of a car in the grocery store parking lot. They sell a lot of cookies.

TUESDAY EVENINGS, SIX THIRTY TO SEVEN

She sat in the church hall basement on the old wooden chair like she'd sat for a thousand Septembers; where a thousand equalled thirty-seven, but seemed like so many more.

In the old days, she'd sat with other women—Tawny Owls, Grey Owls, Brown Owls—chatting and laughing and joyfully waiting for the new girls. Some girls raced down the stairs, leaving mothers or older sisters behind, thrilled to finally be old enough. Some descended slowly, deliberately, holding onto an adult hand, shy and unsure.

For the last eight years, she'd waited alone, but the girls still came. Less of them, sure, but she didn't need many— three or four eight-year-olds to join her nine-year-olds to replace those girls who had flown up. But both of last year's eight-year-olds had moved away, so this year, there were no nine-year-olds.

She watched the clock, watched eight o'clock come and go, and she stayed just a little longer. Sometimes parents got off work late. Or the girls might have school functions they needed to attend.

Eight thirty came and went.

She knew. She could feel the certainty catch at the back of her throat every time she swallowed. No one was going to come. What few girls the right age there were among the greying population of this small town had too many other enticements. Five hundred channels. A hundred gigabytes. Baseball. Ballet. Soccer. Music lessons.

They'd wanted her to fold the troop last year.

Maybe they'd been right.

She reached out a hand to scoop up the paperwork and brochures spread out on the scarred desk in front of her.

"Oi, Missus! Is this where we sign up?"

Decades of dealing with little girls had given her nerves of steel. Although she'd thought herself alone in the basement and could, in fact, see no evidence to the contrary, she neither started nor shrieked, merely leaned forward and peered over the edge of the desk.

Five men peered up at her. The tallest had to have been less than a metre high or she'd have been able to see the top of his head from her chair. All five wore old-fashioned clothing in varying shades of brown: waistcoats and jackets, loose trousers and cotton shirts, handkerchiefs knotted loosely around tanned necks. All five had brown hair and brown eyes. In fact, they looked remarkably like…

She leaned out a little further, half afraid she'd see hairy feet.

Thank God. Brown shoes.

"Take a picture," grumbled one. "Lasts longer."

The other four seemed to find that very funny, but even during all the sniggering, not one expectant gaze had left her face. They were clearly waiting for her to say something.

All right.

"Sign up for what?" she asked.

The tallest little man sighed. "We're Brownies, ain't we? We heared this is where you sign up."

Suddenly, sitting down seemed like an excellent idea.

"Oi! Where'd she go?"

"I'm thinking she fainted, like. Took one look at your ugly puss and fell right... OW!"

"Don't be daft. If she was on the floor, we could see her."

They had accents; a soft burr on voices that rose and fell like her Uncle Dave's after an evening at the Legion. A clattering that a part of her brain translated as wooden soles against tile—she'd worn wood and leather clogs back in the seventies—and all five came around the corner of the desk. Only four of them were in wooden-soled shoes, the fifth wore modern trainers, although she'd never realized they came in brown.

"Right then, there you are." The tallest folded his arms. "Let's get on with it, we ain't got all night."

"Yes, we do."

"Shut it!" he snapped without turning or unlocking his gaze from her face. "You the Brownie leader, then?"

She had to clear her throat to find her voice. "Yes, but..."

"So what's the problem?"

"You're not..." A rudimentary sense of self-preservation

cut her off before she could finish with *the right kind of Brownies*. "…the kind of Brownies I usually deal with."

Their spokesman folded his arms belligerently, his action mirrored by the other four. "So?"

"This organization is for little girls."

"Little girls?"

"Yes."

"But we're *Brownies!*"

She spread her hands in the universal gesture for *that's not really relevant, and there's nothing I can do about it anyway.*

"But, but…"

A small but hoary fist smacked him on the shoulder. "I told you this'd never work, you great git!"

"Little girls," snorted another.

"It'll never happen for us," sighed a third.

Raised fists fell. Feet lifted to kick settled back onto the ground. A mouthful of damp sleeve was spit slowly out. What had clearly been about to descend into violence, became, instead, five dispirited little men.

Shoulders slumped, they turned away.

"Sorry for bothering you, Missus."

"Wait!" Not until they started to turn did she realize she'd been the one to call them back. After a moment's silent panic, she figured she might as well be hung for a sheep as a lamb, and a moment later decided that might not be the best simile she could have used as a couple of the little men looked like they'd rustled a sheep or two in their day. "If you're already Brownies…"

"If?" A bit of the belligerence returned.

"Sorry. *Since* you're already Brownies, why do you want to join my troop?"

"Why?"

"Yes, why?"

"Right, then." A gnarled finger indicated she should hold that thought, and the Brownies huddled up.

"If she can't help, she doesn't need to know."

"If she knows, maybe she can help."

"But then she'll know too much."

"We could kill her."

"Sure and what century are you living in? We'd have CSI all over us before we could say Killicrankie."

"You know, I've never understood why we'd say Killicrankie. It's daft. Totally bloody daft."

"Oh, shut your pie hole."

She wondered if they knew or cared she could hear every word. A short scuffle later, the vote to tell her went four to one. After the forceful application of a clog to the dissenter's nether regions, it ended five votes in favour. As they jumped up to sit on the edge of the desk...

"Right, then, that's a mite easier on the back of the neck."

...she handed out tissues and fished a box of last season's classic cookies out of her bag. All hands were still busy blotting bloody noses and minor bites, so she left the open box on the desk, took a chocolate and a vanilla, and sat back in her chair.

The tallest Brownie gave her a thoughtful look—his shiner already beginning to fade—took a cookie of each flavour, and passed the box along. "It's like this, Missus," he said, "we're tired of being Brownies..."

"All the cleaning."

"And the serving."

"And the not being appreciated."

"Or believed in."

"…and we heard you can make us something else."

"Something else?"

"That's what we heard." He tapped a fingertip to the side of one hirsute nostril.

"Well, my girls fly up to be Guides, but…"

"Guides!" Unsurprisingly, his smile was missing a couple of teeth. "Then that's what we'll be. We'll be Guides."

Agreement from the others emerged slightly muffled by the cookies.

She thought she was taking this remarkably well, all things considered. "You don't understand; Guides are another level in a worldwide organization."

"Aye. And we're Brownies."

"You'll be making us Guides," added the Brownie in the running shoes.

They really weren't getting it. "It's not *Guides* the same way that you're Brownies. It's more a name given to acknowledge that the girls are ready to move on."

"Aye." The tallest Brownie nodded. "And so are we."

"Past ready."

"Way past."

"Long past."

"Oi, Missus! Got any more cookies?"

"No. You've eaten the whole box, any more and you'll make yourself sick." When they accepted that without argument, she took a deep breath and tried again. "Brownies are part of an all-female organization. They're eight- and nine-year-old girls. You're not girls, and even if you were, you'd be too old."

"But we *are* Brownies."

"Yes, but…"

"Que Sera."

"He starts to sing, I'm for stuffin' my fist down his gullet."

"That'd improve things."

"What's he gotta use them fancy foreign words for any-ways?"

"Too big for his bloody britches."

"Stop it." To her surprise, they did—if not immediately, after only some minor bruising. "That kind of behaviour is not good citizenship."

"What does that mean when it's home?"

But the tallest answered before she could. "It means she's taken us on; doesn't it, Missus?"

The clock showed twenty past nine. They were alone in the basement, just her and five Brownies.

"Yes," she told them. "That's what it means." After all, the latest Strategic Plan listed increasing the diversity of membership as a key priority.

❅

Their names were Big Tam, Little Tam, Callum, Conner, and Ewan. There was a reason they sounded like her Uncle Dave.

"Have you looked in your phone book lately," Big Tam snorted. "Two pages of Mc's and near three of Mac's, plus Campbells and Buchanans and Browns and Kerrs. We came across the big pond with them, didn't we. Course, Ewan's working for a Singh now, his last Campbell married over."

Ewan grinned. "I'll take a nice curry over a bloody bowl of milk and a bannock any night."

When she pointed to the curse cup, he sighed and dropped in a coin. She didn't ask where he got the money. She suspected she didn't want to know.

Only Callum, the Brownie in the running shoes, could read and write. The others thought he was full of himself and too quick to take up newfangled ideas. After three fights and a small fire no one would admit to setting, she'd taken the registration forms away and told them she'd fill them in herself. It was important to register them. If they weren't registered then they weren't *real* Brownies, and it would mean nothing when they flew up. She'd feminized their names and added Scottish family names for everyone except for Ewan—who became Eula. He was a Singh. Over the years, she'd helped fill in enough of these forms that the lies came easily.

Too easily, considering that honesty was a part of the Brownie law.

I'll sell extra cookies to make up for it.

The registration fee was $75 dollars each.

"Bugger that!"

Big Tam grabbed Conner by the collar and hauled him back into the circle. "You want to be serving 'til the end of time, then? You want to spend eternity cookin' and cleanin' and muckin' out their shite and grinding their flour? Well, there's not much flour grinding of late, but you take my meaning." He shook the smaller Brownie so hard a confused-looking squirrel fell out of his pocket. "Hand it over," he commanded as Conner grabbed the squirrel and tucked it back out of sight.

She had to drive into the city to sell some of the registration money at a rare coin store. Even considering that half of what they'd offered her had disappeared when the sun hit it, she had more than enough to cover the fees for all five and order each of them a badge vest. Back in her day, they'd have been wearing skorts and knee socks, and, as imagination supplied the visuals, she thanked God that uniform choices had become more flexible.

They met every Tuesday evening in the church hall basement. She intended to run this troop the way she'd run every troop—well, except for the curse cup. That was an idea she'd picked up from a Guide leader who dealt with a very rough group of inner-city tweens.

"Oi, Missus! What's with the sodding mushroom?"

She waited until his coin hit the curse cup before she answered. "It's not a mushroom, it's a toadstool, and it's very old."

"Old?" Conner scoffed, right index finger buried knuckle deep in his nose. "I got boogers older than that there."

"It's old," she repeated. The toadstool had spent every Tuesday evening in the basement for as long as she had. It had been the focus of thousands of circles of girls.

Big Tam stared at her for a long moment. "It's no' old to us."

"But you don't want to be you anymore, do you?"

His brows dipped so deep they met over his nose. "You're daft, Missus."

"Probably." But she was going to turn these Brownies into Guides. That's why they'd come to her, and that's what she did. "Each of you take a cushion and sit in a circle around the toadstool. Oh, and stop calling me Missus. Address me as Brown Owl."

Their reactions put another seventy-five cents, two doubloons, and a farthing in the curse cup, although she'd had to guess that Little Tam's tirade was obscene since she was unfamiliar with all of the words and half the gestures.

It was a small circle, she realized when they were seated, the smallest she'd ever had.

"Don't be worrying about that, Missus," Callum told her reassuringly when she voiced the observation. "Size don't matter."

"You'd say that, would you?" Big Tam snorted, leaping to his feet and reaching into his trousers. "Them what says that, they ain't got size enough to matter. Now, me, what I got…"

"Put it away."

"But…"

"Now."

"Fine. Still bigger," he muttered, sitting down.

Never let them know they'd flustered you. Little girls reacted to weakness like wolves—which was not particularly fair to wolves, who were, on the whole, noble creatures. But saying that little girls reacted to weakness like chickens, who were known to peck their companions to death, didn't have the same kind of mythic power behind it, even though it was more biologically accurate.

"Missus?"

Right.

She cleared her throat and dried her palms on her thighs. "We'll start with the Brownie law."

"Well," Conner said thoughtfully, "we ain't allowed to be rewarded for our services."

"Though that's really more of a guideline than an actual law," Ewan pointed out.

Little Tam nodded. "You're supposed to be leaving stuff out for us."

"Good stuff," Callum qualified. "No shite."

"And a little appreciation for services rendered, that don't go amiss," Big Tam added, to a chorus of: "Oh, aye."

She absolutely was not thinking of what service Big Tam could render. "This is a different Brownie law, for the kinds of Brownies who become Guides."

"Let's have it then, Missus. Owl. Missus Owl."

Close enough.

❋

They learned the law and the promise, and could soon recite them both.

"Honest and kind? This lot?" Conner pulled his finger from his nose and stared at the tip. "That's a laugh."

"You calling me a liar, you miserable little shite?"

"You want kind? Have a knuckle sandwich!"

"I'm gonna feed you my friggin' boot!"

"Up yours, asswipe!"

She got the toadstool back in essentially one piece, and, as she disinfected it before repainting, figured first aid had better be the initial Key Badge.

The curse cup already held enough money for various

bandages, analgesic creams, and cold packs. It took three weeks for them to stop using the slings to tie each other into anatomically impossible positions, and a week after that to stop eating the creams, but, eventually, they learned how to deal with black eyes, bloody noses, scraped knuckles, wrenched shoulders, and swollen genitalia—the latter a necessary addition to the basic course material.

"Who'd have thought that frozen water'd feel so fine nestled up against the 'nads," Little Tam sighed, adjusting the ice pack.

They sold the Classic Cookies in the fall—the chocolate and vanilla, centre cream cookies stamped with the Guide trefoil. She had regular customers who'd bought boxes for years and didn't care if they came from smiling little girls or scowling little men as long as they got their fix.

New customers found themselves holding boxes in one hand and an empty wallet in the other without being entirely certain how it had happened. She was pleasantly surprised to find that, although a few people were over cookied, no one was ever short changed.

"Brownies are honest," Ewan reminded her, as the entire troop looked a bit insulted by the surprised part of her reaction.

She made it up to them by presenting *Money Talk* badges all around.

They were heading for a record year when she realized they were in danger of attracting too much attention. "You've done remarkably well," she said, choosing to ignore the baby swapped for a doll made of cookies that she'd managed to swap back just in time. "But record numbers will bring us to provincial attention, maybe even national, and Brownies are supposed to be secretive folk, who keep out of sight."

"No one saw us, Missus Owl."

"But they'll know something is going on, and someone will come to investigate."

"Ah," Little Tam nodded. "CSI."

They all watched too much television, but she'd dealt with that before. The best way to counteract it was to lead them into the limitless worlds of imagination that came with books.

Half an hour of every meeting was devoted to teaching four of her five brownies how to read; unfortunately, without much success.

"It's not that they don't want to learn, Missus Owl," Callum confided after the other four had vanished from the basement muttering about just what they'd like to do to Dick and Jane. "It's just you gotta teach them from stories they're interested in."

"Myths and legends?"

He snorted. "Not quite."

❄

"Dear Penthouse forum. Last night when my girlfriend and I were getting…"

"Sound it out, Little Tam."

"Int. I. Mate. Intimate!"

"Very good."

"Hey! Let's see them pictures!"

"Back off! It's my turn to read!"

"Git!"

"Arse!"

"Who remembers how to apply the ice pack?"

For the Halloween meeting, she dressed as an Indian Princess. She always dressed as an Indian Princess; the costume had moved past traditional some years earlier and was approaching legendary. This year, the beaded, buckskin dress felt restrictive and uninspiring, but it was too late to change.

Big Tam dressed up as a Boggart, Little Tam as a Hobgoblin, Conner as a Bodach, Ewan as a Red Cap, and Callum, always a bit more progressive than the others, as Liza Minnelli. His story about her comeback concert was terrifying.

In November, they used the kitchen upstairs in the church hall to bake a Sugar Pie.

"Or, as the Acadians call it," she told them as Big Tam sprinkled cream on the maple sugar, "*la tarte au sucre.*"

The old oven was a bit temperamental and she had to call the minister's wife over to help get it going. The Brownies stayed out of sight—she explained they were down in the basement working on a project—and didn't reappear until the minister's wife was gone and the pie was in the oven.

While it baked, they traced the route of the dispossessed Acadian exiles out on a map.

She cut the pie into small pieces, but that hardly mattered when everyone had seconds. And thirds.

That night, persons unknown repaved the parking lot behind the town hall, causing incidental damage to five pigeons and 1988 Buick. The pigeons recovered, the owner of the Buick found a bag of assorted coin worth twice the Blue Book value of the car in his trunk, and she resolved to be more careful with sugar in the future.

By mid-December, the curse cup held three hundred and twelve dollars and forty-two cents as well as three wizened, black beans Conner swore were magic and should cover his contributions well into the new year.

"Oi! None of that, ya cheap bastard!"

Later, after a review of first aid basics, she suggested they use the money to help under-privileged children celebrate Christmas.

"We don't do Christmas," Big Tam pointed out. "We're older than that, ain't we."

"Aren't we. And I'm not asking you to do Christmas. I'm asking you to help children. Think of it as service to the community."

"We're all about service to the bleedin' community, Missus Owl."

"Workin' our arses off in the background, never getting no recognition."

"Aye, and we're right tired of it."

She could understand that.

"Still," Callum added a moment later, "it ain't the kiddies' fault."

Three in the backseat, two with her in the front, and she could fit all five into her car for a trip to the big toy store in the city.

"Big Tam, take your hand off my thigh."

"Sorry, Missus Owl. Ewan's shoving like."

"Bugger I am!"

"Brownies, what did we discuss about seatbelts?"

"No one gets punched," five voices responded. "No one gets bit. Seatbelts stay on, and no one gets hit."

"But…"

"No, Ewan."

"Not fair, Missus Owl! He sodding started it."

They had three hundred and twenty-seven dollars to spend by the time they reached the store.

She ran into the minister's wife as she emerged from a painfully pink aisle, her arms piled high with boxed baby dolls.

"Are you here on your own?" the minister's wife asked, as she helpfully adjusted the pile.

"No, I'm here with my Brownies."

"I'd love to meet them." Smile tight and official, the minister's wife peered around the store. "Where are they?"

From three aisles away she heard, "Sod off, you cheap bastard. We're buying the web-slinging set what comes with Doc Octopus."

"Oh, they're around."

Little Tam was the hit of the talent show in January. The other four stomped and shouted and whistled, applauding long and loudly when he finished his song. Unfortunately, it was in Gaelic and she didn't understand a word of it.

"It's about a shepherd," Big Tam explained, glaring around the circle as though daring the others to contradict him. "A shepherd what really, really loves his sheep."

❋

In February, on the Tuesday evening closest to the full moon, they made snow men—one large and five small—out behind the church hall. She provided carrots for noses, but each of the Brownies had been told to bring enough small stones to create eyes and mouth.

"What's so funny, mate?" Callum muttered, finishing his snowman's smile. "I'm freezing my bloody bollocks off out here."

"This is a part of your Winter Outside badge," she reminded him, uncertain if bollocks was cursing or slang.

"Is there an icicle up the arse badge? Because I've got that one nailed."

The minister's wife appeared as she was unlocking her car.

"I've missed them again, have I?"

"Only just." She smiled and checked to make sure that she'd obliterated the distinctive prints made by hobnailed boots.

"I could see you from my upstairs window." The minister's wife gestured toward the old stone house that went with the church. "I couldn't see your Brownies, though."

"I expect the angle was wrong. And that pine tree's in the way."

"I've never seen them." The light over the parking lot made her eyes look a little wild. "I see you park here every Tuesday evening, but never them."

"They come in through the other entrance." She didn't

know what entrance they came through; they arrived every week a few minutes after she did. The *other* entrance was therefore no lie. "You've come out without your boots and hat. You do know you lose forty-five percent of your body heat through an uncovered head, don't you? You should get back inside before you get a chill."

Her first year as a leader, she'd brought in pictures of John Glenn, her Great Aunt Rose, who'd raised eight children on her own after her husband had been killed in the First World War, and Wonder Woman. She'd talked about what it meant to be a hero and then had the girls come up with heroes of their own. Over the years, she'd added many of their heroes to her portfolio. This year, it took her nearly an hour to carefully tape them all to the painted concrete walls.

She hadn't been snuck up on in thirty-seven years, and so she turned, smiling, when she heard the faint sound of footsteps behind her. The tall, dark-haired woman with the minister's wife came as a bit of shock, but she didn't let it show. It helped that, over the last little while, she'd become used to seeing the minister's wife pop up at odd moments. "Good evening. May I help you?"

The dark-haired woman held out her hand. "Hello, my name is Janet O'Neill." Under her coat, a blue and white striped shirt, a dark blue sweater, a prominent pin… "I'm from the provincial office."

Of course she was.

"I was in the area visiting Samantha Jackson…"

The name threw her for a moment, and then she remembered.

Samantha Jackson was the minister's wife, who was looking less nervous than usual now she had backup.

"…and I thought I'd drop in and visit your troop."

"My troop."

"Your Brownies."

Oh, dear.

"I see you're studying heroes tonight. Why don't you run us through the pictures while we wait for the girls to arrive?"

It took forty-five minutes. It would have taken longer, but after forty-five minutes, Janet raised her hand and said, "They're not coming are they?"

"Well, of course they…"

"Aren't!" the minister's wife finished dramatically. "I've never seen these Brownies of yours. No one has. I've asked around, and no one in town has enrolled their daughter in the program."

"You've spoken to everyone in town?" She was honestly curious. Who knew the minister's wife had that much free time.

"Not everyone. A lot of people, though. It's a small town!"

Janet pulled five familiar registration forms from her brief-case. "I just want to ask you a few questions about these forms. You filled them in yourself, didn't you?"

"Yes, but only because they couldn't."

"There is no they!" The minister's wife jabbed a shaking finger at her. "No one came to register that night, but you've been a Brownie leader since the beginning of time and you couldn't bear not having a troop. So you made them up, didn't you? They're total figments of your imagination!"

"They are not!"

"Then where are they?"

"They won't come when you're here!"

"Why not?"

"Why should they? You don't believe in them."

Janet cleared her throat.

She stepped back, took a deep breath, and apologized for shouting.

"I need to meet these girls," Janet said firmly. "I need to know that our organization hasn't been…"

"Used by a crazy lady!" the minister's wife finished.

"I swear to you," she spoke directly to Janet, "my Brownies may be a little rough around the edges, but they're trying, and isn't that what we're about? They're doing their best, and they understand about duty…"

"Duty hasn't been a part of the promise for years," Janet reminded her gently.

"Well, maybe it should be. The point is, they want to be more than they are and they came to me for help, and I helped them because that's what we're about too. Helping."

"I need to meet these girls," Janet repeated. "Or I'm afraid that…"

"Oi, Missus. Sorry we're late."

Hobnailed boots coming down the stairs. In front as usual, Big Tam held out a gnarled hand to Janet O'Neill. "Tammy McGregor," he said. "Pleased to meetcha, Missus. This here's my younger sister, Tina." Little Tam grunted, still apparently annoyed he'd had to change his name. "Our Da gives us all a ride into town, but he had a cow in calf and we couldn't go until the bugger popped."

"Oh, I didn't realize you were all from farms."

She blinked. If that was the provincial leader's only concern, she was adding a new picture to her wall of heroes.

"Well, Eula here ain't…"

Ewan waved.

"…but Da picks her up on the edge of town. We'd all been part of 4-H, but we had to keep Karen away from the sheep, if you know what I mean; wink-wink, nudge-nudge."

"Oi, none of that you lying bastard!"

She cleared her throat. Callum stopped his charge, sighed, and tossed a coin in the curse cup, muttering, "Knuckle sandwich later, boyo."

Conner sidled up to Janet, and tugged on her sleeve. "I learned to read here."

"Well, good for you."

"I got a badge for it."

"Congratulations." Her pleasure seemed genuine.

"But there's no one there!"

Everyone turned to stare at the minister's wife, who had collapsed into a chair and was visibly shaking.

"She takes a header, dibs on mouth-to-mouth!"

"I'm for CPR, me!"

"You just wants ta grab her boobies."

"Brownies!"

The rush toward the minister's wife stopped cold.

"With me, please. Let Guider O'Neill handle this."

They muttered, but they fell in behind her as Janet eased the minister's wife up out of the chair.

"Come on, Mrs. Jackson. I'll just take you home now, and maybe we'll make a few phone calls, all right?" Half way up the stairs, the smaller woman supported against her shoulder, she turned and smiled. "It was lovely to meet you all. And I'm sorry for the misunderstanding."

"Nice lady, that," Ewan announced as the outside door closed.

"It's called a glamour," Big Tam explained, before she could ask. "The dark one, for all she was here to check you out, truly wanted to see Brownies, so that's what she saw and heard—wee girls. The other, well, she'd convinced herself that there were no such thing as Brownies, hadn't she? So that's all she saw."

"It's not quite a lie," Callum added.

They watched anxiously for her reaction.

"You're not responsible for people's expectations, but," she added as they began to preen, "it is important that people not have low expectations of you, and I don't think you can get lower than Mrs. Jackson's."

Little Tam nodded. "No expectations at all, I'd say that's lower than an ant's arse."

"I think it would be a good troop project to raise those expectations."

By summer, the minister's wife had gotten used to a spotless house, clean clothes, cooked meals, and landscaping the envy of the neighbourhood. She started a Pilates course, had an affair with the UPS driver, and seemed a lot happier.

The Brownies picked up two more badges.

They couldn't go to camp…

"Glamour a great group of little girls? No offence, Missus, but are you daft?"

…so they learned about the wonders of nature by hiking together in the woods outside of town.

She learned there were unicorns in the woods.

"Why is it they won't come to you, Missus Owl?"

"That's none of your business, Big Tam."

They gathered to watch the Perseid meteor shower for their Key to Stem badge.

"Make a wish, Missus Owl."

"It's not a falling star, Ewan. It's a piece of rock burning up in the atmosphere."

"Make a wish anyway."

So she did.

They got their Key to the Living World badge by joining the fall Trash Bash and cleaning up a full five kilometres of road.

"It doesn't count as trash if it's parked in someone's garage, Conner."

"But it's a Lada, Missus Owl."

"Put it back."

Callum got his Pet Pals badge by directing the dump rats in a performance of West Side Story. It was the best amateur theatre she'd seen in years.

That Halloween, she dressed as a Gypsy. Big Tam was a Leprechaun, Little Tam a Fianna, Conner a Jack-in-Irons, Ewan a Phouka, and Callum came as Britney Spears, circa *Hit Me, Baby, One More Time.*

At Christmas, they delivered gift baskets to the seniors at Markam Manner. The Brownies picked out the contents themselves. Since the seniors seemed to appreciate being treated as adults instead of grey-haired children, she decided to consider the baskets a success. The staff of the nursing home were less accepting, but they were the ones dealing with the aftereffects.

By spring, all five vests were covered in badges—all the key badges and all but two of the interest badges. There were no Sparks for them to help—not necessarily a bad thing—and as they'd tried and failed to hack CSIS on her laptop, she'd refused to give them their *Information Technology* badge on principle.

Most leaders kept their troops intact until the end of summer, so the girls could have one more visit to camp, but since that was still out of the question, she decided they should fly up in the spring.

She liked the symbolism better; new growth, new life, and the same ceremony her old Brown Owl had used when she'd flown up.

The Brownies appeared, as they always did, a few moments

after she'd set the toadstool in place. They recited the Law and the Promise and, with a minimal amount of insults and no profanity at all, sat down.

She had a whole speech prepared, dealing with what it meant to be a Brownie and what it meant to leave that behind and move on, but looking around the circle, from face to face, all that seemed somehow presumptuous. They knew more about what it meant to be a Brownie than she ever would.

So all she said was, "It's time."

They looked a lot like her girls then, a little scared, very excited—quite a bit hairier.

She'd built a three-step platform; shallow steps, so that the top was no more than a foot off the ground. Two posts—broom handles, really—wrapped in sparkly ribbon and attached to the platform, with more ribbon strung between them, made a low door. Hanging from the ribbon were five sets of construction paper butterfly wings.

"Big Tam."

He started, stood, and walked to the first step, tugging his vest into place. She smiled reassuringly, and he nodded.

"Do your best to be honest and kind." A light touch on his shoulder.

One step.

"Be true to yourself."

Two steps.

"Help to take care of the world around you."

He was on the platform now.

"Take your wings and fly."

She'd written their names on the construction paper in lavender glitter ink. A little girly maybe, but old habits were hard to break.

Big Tam reached for his wings, took a deep breath, and, without looking back, jumped through the door.

The way he disappeared into a soft white light that smelled of fresh-mown hay came as no great surprise. The brass band playing *She'll be Coming Round the Mountain*, well, that was a little unsettling, but she coped.

Little Tam. Callum. Conner. Ewan. Who paused on the platform and said, "Thank you."

"You're welcome."

Alone in the basement of the church hall, she reached up to take the ribbon down and shrieked as Big Tam's head appeared between the broom handles, the first time in thirty-seven years she'd been taken by surprise.

"Oi, Missus. You comin'?"

"I'm not…"

Over the sound of a euphonium solo, she heard: "Oi! Get yer flamin' mitts of me wings!"

"I'll wing you, ya skeezy pervert!"

"You'd best bring the ice pack," Big Tam sighed as he disappeared.

She scooped it out of the cooler, picked up the curse cup, and climbed to the top of the platform. As she ducked under the ribbon, she wondered if her old wings still worked…

When Julie Czerneda asked for submissions for her anthology *Mythsprings,* she wanted them based on the Canadian myths and stories, poems and songs that inspired us.

For most of my life, I have lived near the Great Lakes—not on, waterfront property is insanely expensive, but near enough to walk to the shore. My father used to run a diving school. Every summer through my teens, a friend and I would go to her family's cottage in the Thousand Islands and canoe out to watch the lake freighters pass. I was at university in Thunder Bay the year Gordon Lightfoot came out with the *Wreck of the Edmund Fitzgerald,* and the local DJ played it every morning at 7:30, right after my alarm went off. Which is to say, the lakes and I have history.

The ships and their stories within this story are true.

Diana and Sam, and the mythos they operate in, are from my three volume Keeper Chronicles—*Summon the Keeper*, *The Second Summoning*, and *Long Hot Summoning*. You should be able to follow the story even if you haven't read them, but, if you haven't, they're now available as a trade omnibus.

UNDER SUMMONS

Eyes squinted against the early morning sun, Diana Hansen walked down the lane toward the Waupoos Marina listening to the string of complaints coming from the cat in her backpack.

"The boat is leaving at seven thirty," she said when he finally paused for breath. "If we'd gotten up any later, we'd have missed it."

The head and front paws of a marmalade tabby emerged through the open zipper and peered over Diana's shoulder toward the marina. "I thought need provided for Keepers during a Summoning?"

"Need has provided, Sam. There's a boat leaving for Main Duck Island this morning."

He snorted. "Why can't need provide a boat at a reasonable hour?"

"It doesn't work that way. Besides, cats do that hunt at dusk and dawn thing—you should be happy to be up."

"First of all, I'm not hunting. And second," he added ducking down into the backpack as a car passed them, "I'd rather have sausages for breakfast than a damp mouse."

"Who wouldn't."

Another car passed, bouncing from pot hole to pot hole.

"You'd better stay down," Diana told him, hooking her thumbs under the padded shoulder straps. "It's starting to get busy."

"Oh yeah," the cat muttered as a pickup truck followed the two cars. "It's a real rush hour. I'll be napping, if you need me."

The Ministry of Natural Resources trawler was tied up at the nearer of the big piers out behind the marina. Pausing at the south-west corner of the big grey building, Diana scoped out the crowd. Most of the twenty-four other travellers were older couples, sensibly dressed in long pants, wearing both hiking boots and hats. Half a dozen women were obviously together, and, just as obviously, part of a club—unless they'd all accidentally worn the same lime-green t-shirt. There was a sprinkling of younger adults, and three teenagers. Two girls, probably sisters, and a boy. They were the only people wearing shorts. The boy caught her gaze and smirked. He was a good-looking kid—and he knew it.

"Okay, everyone, listen up!" A fortyish man wearing Ministry khaki, climbed up on a wooden crate and waved a clipboard. "Some of you already know me, but for the rest, I'm Gary Straum, and I'll be your guide this trip. The young man driving the boat is Jamie Wierster. He knows almost as much as I do about the island, so if I'm not available, he'll do his best to tell you anything you need to know."

A ruddy-cheeked, young giant leaned out of the tiny cabin and waved.

"I just want to remind you of a few things before we get started," Gary continued as the two girls giggled. "Main Duck Island is part of the St. Lawrence Islands National Parks system and is a nature sanctuary. You may not take samples of the plant life away with you—this means no picking, no digging, no collecting seeds. The wildlife is to be left strictly alone. If there's a disagreement of any kind between you and any creature living on that island, I will rule in favour of the creature. Anything you carry in must be carried out. If you can't live with that, I suggest you leave now." Gary smiled as an older man grabbed the back of the teenage boy's skater shirt and hauled him back by his side. "All right, then. When I read your name, come and pick up your life jacket..." He gestured at the open steel locker beside him. "...put it on, and board. The sooner we get going, the more time we'll have to spend on the island."

Diana's name was the last on the list. She hadn't put it there, and she felt a little sorry for the actual twenty-fifth person, who'd been bumped to make room for her, but there was a hole in the fabric of reality out on Main Duck Island and it was her job as a Keeper to close it.

Feeling awkward and faintly ridiculous in the life jacket, Diana sat down on a wooden bench and set her backpack carefully at her feet.

"I saw the cat. When we passed you in the lane."

She answered the teenage boy's smile with one of her own as he dropped onto the bench beside her. According to the boarding list, his name was Ryan. Ryan, like everyone else on the boat, was a Bystander, and given the relative numbers, Keepers were used to working around them. "Of course you did, Ryan. *Please* forget about it."

It really was a magic word.

He frowned. Looked around like he was wondering why he'd sat beside her, and after mumbling something inarticulate, moved across the boat to sit back down in his original seat. The girls, Mackenzie and Erin, sitting on the bench in front of him, giggled.

"I get the impression you're not the giggling type."

It was one of the older women, her husband busy taking pictures of Gary casting off and jumping aboard.

"Not really, no."

"Carol Diamond. That's my husband Richard. We're here as part of an Elder Hostel program." Her wave took in the rest of the hats-and-hiking-boots crowd. "All of us."

"Great."

"Are you travelling on your own, dear?"

"Yes, I am."

Carol smiled the even, white smile of the fully-dentured and nodded toward the teenagers. "Well, how nice you have some people of your own age to spend time with."

Diana blinked. Two months shy of twenty, she did not appreciate being lumped in with the children. Fortunately, between the motor and the wind it was difficult to carry on a casual conversation, and Carol didn't try, content to sit quietly while her husband took pictures of Waupoos Island, Prince Edward Point, waves, sky, gulls, the other people in the boat, and once, while he was fiddling with the focus, his lap.

The three pictures with Diana in them would be mysteriously over-exposed.

So would one of the shots he'd taken of the southern view across Lake Ontario, but Diana had nothing to do with that.

"Hey!" Ryan managed to make himself heard over the ambient noise. "What's that?"

Everyone squinted in the direction he was pointing. A series of small, dark dots rose above a sharp-edged horizon.

"That's our first sight of the island; we're about five miles out." Gary moved closer to the teenager. "Well done."

Ryan turned just far enough to scowl at him. "Not that. Closer to us."

About twenty metres from the boat, another series of small dark dots rose and fell with the slight chop. Then, suddenly, they were gone. The last dot rose up into a triangular point just before it disappeared.

"That looked like a tail!"

"Might be a loon," Gary offered.

"Fucking big loon!"

"Ryan!"

Ryan rolled his eyes at his father, but muttered an apology.

"It's probably just some floating junk." A half-turn included the rest of the group in the discussion. "You'd be amazed at the stuff we find out here." His list had almost everyone laughing.

Lake monster wasn't on it, Diana noted.

As Main Duck Island coalesced into a low, solid line of trees with a light house rising off the westernmost point, Gary explained that it had been acquired by the park service in 1998, having been previously owned by John Foster Dulles, a prominent lawyer who'd been American Secretary of State in the Eisenhower administration. The island was 209 hectares in size, and except for the ruins of some old fishing cabins that had been posted *no trespassing*, none of it was off limits.

"The lighthouse?" one of the lime-green t-shirt group asked.

"Is unmanned and closed to the public, but you can go right up to it and poke around."

Mention of the lighthouse started the shipwreck stories. There were a lot of them; the area around the island was known as the graveyard of Lake Ontario and contained the wrecks of two- and three-masted schooners, brigantines, barges, and steamers, dating back to a small French warship en route to Fort Niagara with supplies and a pay chest of gold for the troops that went down in late fall around 1750.

Diana had begun to get a bad feeling about the location of the hole she had to close.

As Jamie steered the trawler into School House Bay, Gary told the story of the *John Randall*. She'd anchored in the bay for shelter back in 1920, only to have the wind shift to the north and drive her ashore. Her stern hit a rock, her engine lifted, and she broke in two.

"The crew of four scrambled up onto the bow and remained there for ten hours, washed by heavy seas and lashed by a November northeaster. They finally made it ashore on a hatch cover and stayed with the lighthouse keeper nine days before they were picked up. You can still see the wooden ribs and planks of the ship in the bay."

"So no one died?" Ryan asked.

"Not that time." With the dock only metres away, Gary moved over to the port side of the boat and picked up the rear mooring line. "But a year and eight days later, the Captain of the *Randall* went down while in command of the *City of New York*. His wife and his ten-month-old daughter went to the bottom with him."

"So sad," Carol sighed as Gary leapt out onto the dock. "But at least they were together." She twisted on the bench to look back the way they'd come. "I bet those waves hide a hundred stories."

"I bet they hide a hundred and one," Diana muttered, hoisting her backpack. She was not going to enjoy explaining this to Sam.

❋

"In the water?"

"Essentially."

Sam's ears saddled. "How *essentially*?" The echoed word dripped with feline sarcasm.

"Under the water."

"Have a nice time."

Down on one knee beside him, Diana stroked along his back and out his tail. "There's a lake monster out there, too. Looked like a sea serpent. Probably came through the hole."

"And that's supposed to make me change my mind?" the cat snorted. He peered off the end of the dock into the weedy bay. "Frogs pee in that water, you know."

"That's not..." She probed at the Summons, trying to narrow it down a little. "...exactly the water we're going into."

He sat back and looked up at her, amber eyes narrowed. "What water are we going into, exactly? If *we* were going, that is?"

"Southwest." She straightened. "Toward the lighthouse."

"I'll wait here."

"Come on. The nature hike went through the woods. We'll take the beach and avoid an audience." About to lift the backpack, she paused. "You want to walk or ride?"

Tail tip twitching, he shoved past her, muttering, "What part of I'll wait here did you not understand?"

The beach consisted of two to three metres of smooth gravel, trimmed with a ridge of polished zebra mussel shells at the edge of the water. As Diana and Sam rounded a clump of sumac, they saw Ryan, a garter snake wrapped around one hand, moving quietly toward the two girls crouched at the ridge of shells.

"You think we should get involved?" Sam wondered.

Before Diana could answer, Ryan placed his foot wrong, the gravel rattled, and both girls turned. Although he no longer had surprise on his side, he waved the snake in their general direction.

"Look what I have!"

Braced for shrieking and running, Diana was surprised to see both girls advance toward Ryan.

"How dare you!" Mackenzie snapped, fists on her hips. "How would you like it if someone picked you up by the throat and flailed you at people?"

"The poor snake!" Erin added.

"I'm not hurting it," Ryan began, but Mackenzie ran right over his protest with her opinion of the kind of people who abused animals for fun, while Erin gently took the snake from him and released it.

"In answer to your question," Diana snickered as they started walking again, "I don't think we're needed."

A little further down the beach, two even larger snakes lay tangled together in the sun on a huge slab of flat rock. The female hissed as they went by. Sam hissed back.

"Don't be rude, Sam, it's their beach."

"She started it," Sam muttered.

About half way to the lighthouse, with the teenagers out of sight behind them, Diana headed for the water.

"Is it here?"

"No, it's farther west, but these shoals go out over half a mile in places, and I'd rather not be visible from shore for that long. I don't want to have to maintain a misdirection when we're wading waist deep."

"When *we're* wading?" Sam sniffed disdainfully at the mussel shells. "Lift me over this, would you."

"Actually," she bent and picked him up, settling his weight against her chest, "why don't I just carry you until we're in the water."

"Yeah, yeah." He sighed and adjusted his position slightly. "It's going to be cold."

"It's Lake Ontario, I don't think it ever gets warm. But don't worry, you won't feel it." As the water lapped against the beach gravel a centimetre from the toes of her shoes, Diana reached into the Possibilities and wrapped power around them. Then she stepped forward. "There's a nice, wide channel here," she said, moving carefully over the flat rock. Sam would be completely unbearable if she missed her footing and a wave knocked them down. "We can follow the rift out to deep water and..."

The bottom dropped out from under her feet.

She stopped their descent before the channel grew uncomfortably narrow. The last thing she wanted was to get her foot stuck between two rocks while under three metres of Lake Ontario with a cranky cat. Well, maybe not the *last* thing she wanted—being forced to sit through a marathon viewing of Question Period ranked higher on the list, but not by much.

Thanks to the zebra mussels, the water was remarkably clear—the one benefit of an invasive species that blocked intake pipes up and down the Great Lakes. Enough light made it down from the surface that they could easily see their way.

"Of course, *I* could see anyway," Sam reminded her as she let him go. He swam slowly around her, hair puffing out from his body. "Cats see much better than humans in low light levels." A little experimentation proved he could use his tail as a rudder. "You know, when you don't have to get wet, swimming is kind of fun. Hey! Is that a fish?"

Since the fish was moving in the right direction, and Sam didn't have a hope of catching it, Diana merely followed along behind, half her attention on the Summons, and the other half on the cat.

"Sam, come on! This way! We've got to go deeper."

"How deep?" he demanded, scattering a small school of herring.

"Right to the bottom." She slipped one arm out of her backpack and swung it around so she could pull out her flashlight. "Come on, and stop bothering the fish."

"Something has them freaked."

"They probably don't get a lot of cats down here."

"I don't think it's me. Mostly, I seem to be confusing them."

"Welcome to the club."

"What?"

"Never mind." The water was definitely getting darker. Jade green now and, finally, a little murky. "If it's not you, then what?"

"Something big."

"The sea serpent?"

He was back at her side so quickly that the impact sent her spinning slowly counter-clockwise. "Maybe."

Diana stopped the spin before her third revolution. A Keeper spinning three times counter-clockwise near an open accident site could have unpleasant—or, at the very least unlikely—consequences.

"How can you have a sea serpent in a lake?" Sam snorted in a tone that said very clearly, *I wasn't scared, so don't think for a moment I was.*

Diana shrugged. "I don't know. I guess because lake serpent sounds dumb."

"What's that?"

She turned the beam of the flashlight. A small piece of metal glinted on a narrow shelf of rock. "We should check it out."

"Is it part of the Summons?"

"Yes... No..." She started to swim. "Maybe." Feeling the faint tug of a current nearer the rocks, she half turned. "Stay close. I don't want you swept away."

He paddled a little faster and tucked up against her side. "Good. I don't want to *be* swept away."

"We're lucky it's so calm today. On a rough day with high waves, there's probably a powerful undertow through here."

"Don't want to be eaten by an under-toad," Sam muttered.

"Not under-toad. Undertow."

"You sure of that?"

Glancing down into the dark depths of the lake, Diana wasn't, so, to be on the safe side, she stopped thinking about it. The older Keepers got unnecessarily shirty about the accidental creation of creatures from folklore. As a general rule, the creatures weren't too happy about it either.

"It's the clasp off a change purse." The leather purse itself had long rotted away. "Hang on..." Slipping two fingers down into a crack in the rock, she pulled out a copper coin, too corroded to be identified further.

"You should put that back."

A second coin. She tucked them both into the front pocket of her jeans.

"Okay, fine. Don't listen to the cat."

"I need them."

"What for?"

Good question. "I don't know yet. Come on."

"Come on?" Sam repeated, paddling with all four feet to keep up. "You say that like I was the one who paused to do a little grave robbing."

"First of all, that wasn't a grave, and second," she continued before Sam could argue, "I haven't actually robbed anything since the coins are still here. In the water."

"In your pocket."

"That only counts if I take them away with me."

"So you've borrowed them?"

"More or less."

"Less," the cat snorted.

Diana let him have the last word. It was pretty much the only way to shut him up.

By the time they reached the bottom, the only illumination came from the flashlight. The water was a greenish-yellow, small particulates drifting through the path of the beam.

"Are we there yet?"

"A little further west."

The bottom was still mostly rock, but there were patches of dirt supporting a few small weeds in spite of the depth. They followed a low ridge for close to half a kilometre, stopping when it rose suddenly to within a few metres of the surface.

"This is the place," Diana said, sweeping the light over the rock. "Somewhere close and... Sam, what are you doing?"

He was floating motionless, nose-to-nose with a good-sized herring. "Staring contest."

"You can't win."

"Cats always win."

"I don't think fish have eyelids."

Sam's tail started to lash, propelling him forward. "You cheater!"

Diana couldn't be sure, but she thought the fish looked slightly sheepish as it turned and darted away. "Never mind that!" she yelled, as Sam took off in pursuit. "We're right on top of the Summons, so I'm thinking—given where we are—that we've got to find a wreck."

"In a minute!" Sam disappeared around the edge of the shoal. "I'm just gonna teach that cheating fish a..."

"Sam?"

"Found it."

"Found what?" Diana demanded as she swam after the cat. "Oh."

Much like Main Duck Island itself, the shoal rose to become a nearly-vertical underwater cliff on the north side, but fell off in layers to the south. On one layer, about a meter and a half up from the bottom, the skeletal prow of an old, wooden ship jutted out from the ridge, huge timbers held in place in the narrow angle between two slabs of canted rock and preserved by the cold of the water.

"Well, this is..."

"Obvious," snorted Sam. "Big hunk of rock rising toward the surface. Exposed wreck. Probably been a hundred divers down here every summer."

"Probably," Diana agreed, swimming closer. "But this is where the hole is, I'm sure of it. Somebody did something sometime recently."

"Oh, that's definitive," Sam sighed, following her in.

The hole she'd been Summoned to close was not part of the wreck, but in the rock beside it, where a narrow crevice cut down into the lake bed.

"Isn't the word hole usually more of a metaphorical description," Sam wondered as Diana floated head down and feet up, peering into the crevice.

"Usually. Still is, mostly." The actual opening between this world and the nastier end of the Possibilities stretched out on both sides of the crevice, but it was centred over the dark, triangular crack in the rock. "There's something down here."

"I'm guessing fish poo."

"And you'd be right."

"Eww."

"But something else, too." Tucking the flashlight under her chin, Diana grabbed onto a rock with her left hand and snaked her right down into the crack. "Almost..."

"If you lose that hand, are you still going to be able to use a can opener?"

"I'm not going to lose the hand!"

"I'm just asking."

Sharp edges of rock dug into her arm as she forced her hand deeper, her jacket riding up away from her wrist. One fingertip touched... something. Even such a gentle pressure moved whatever it was away. A little further. Another touch. She managed to finally hook it between her first two fingers.

"Uh, Diana, about that sea serpent..."

"What about it?" She'd have to move her arm slowly and carefully out of the crack, or she'd lose whatever she was holding.

"It's either heading this way from the other side of the wreck, or the Navy's running a submarine in the Great Lakes."

"I pick option B."

"And you'd be wrong."

Time to yank; she could always pick the thing up again. Unfortunately, a sharp tug didn't free her arm. Bright side, she managed to hang onto the thing. Not-so-bright side, approaching sea serpent.

Wait! If her arm was stuck, then she didn't need to hold the rock, and if she didn't need to hold the rock...

She grabbed the flashlight and aimed the beam toward the wreck, hoping it would be enough. Pulling power from the Possibilities over a hole would not be smart. There were worse things than lake monsters out beyond the edges of reality.

Framed between two rotting timbers, green eyes flashed gold in the light. Mouth gaping, the sea serpent folded back on itself and fled, the final flick of its triangular tail knocking a bit of board off the wreck.

"Looks bigger up close," Diana noted, trying to remember how to breathe.

"You think!" Sam snarled, paws and tail thrashing as he bobbed about in currents stirred up by the creature's passage.

"Maybe it was just curious."

"Sure it was. Because you get that big eating plankton!"

"Whales do."

"*Some* whales do, and that was not a whale! That was a predator. I know a predator when I see one!"

Diana tucked the flashlight back under her chin and reached out to stroke the line of raised hair along Sam's spine—the Possibility that allowed them to move and breathe underwater granting the touch. "You're shouting."

He speared her with an amber gaze. "I don't want to be eaten by a sea serpent."

"Who does?"

"Who cares?" he snapped. "The point is, I don't. Let's get that hole closed and get back on dry land before I'm a canapé."

Diana had to admit he had a point, although she admitted it silently rather than give him more ammunition for complaints. The serpent was about ten metres long and almost a meter in diameter. A five-kilo cat would be barely a mouthful. The sooner she got the hole closed, the better.

Carefully, but as quickly as she could, she worked her right hand out of the crack and, when it was finally free, dropped a fragment of bone into the palm of her left.

"The graveyard of Lake Ontario," Sam noted solemnly, his cinnamon nose nearly touching her hand. "There's more than just ships at rest down here."

"Not every body washed ashore," Diana agreed, with a sigh. "I'm betting there's more of this body down in that crevice."

"You think it got smashed and that's what made the hole?"

"I think someone—probably someone diving around the wreck—smashed it deliberately, and that's what made the hole."

"You need to get the rest of the bone out."

It wasn't a question, but she answered it anyway. "I do."

"Great. Considering how long the first piece took, we're going to be down here forever, and that serpent's going to come back, and it's going to be kitties and bits. You're the bits," he added.

"Thanks, I got that. You're not usually this fatalistic."

"Hello? Lake monster. Cat at the bottom of Lake Ontario."

"You worry too much. Now that I've got one piece out, I can call the rest to it. It'll be fast." She held the hand holding the bone out over the crack and Called. Other fragments floated up, danced in the water, and, after a moment or two, formed most of a human jaw.

Suddenly conscious of being watched, Diana whirled around to see a herring hanging in the water. "What?"

Silver sides flashing, it swam about two metres away then stopped, turned, and continued staring.

"Is that your friend from before?"

"We're not friends," Sam snorted. "Get on with it."

Diana studied the jaw. "There's a tooth missing."

Sam looked from the curved bone to the Keeper. "*A* tooth?"

"Okay, a bunch of teeth and the rest of the skeleton, but right here... see where the reformed jaw is a different shade?" She touched it lightly with the tip of one finger. "There was a tooth in there until recently. Whoever did this cracked the jaw and took the tooth."

"Why?"

"People'll notice if you come up from a dive with most of a jaw, but you can hide a tooth."

Sam licked his shoulder thoughtfully, frowned when his tongue made no impression on his fur because of the Possibilities keeping him dry, and finally said, "Cats don't care about the things we leave behind."

"People do. Disturbing a body—even one this old—in order to get a souvenir is illegal, immoral, and kind of gross. So, now we have a problem."

"The lake monster."

"No."

Before she could continue, Sam shifted so he was almost vertical in the water and pointed upwards with one front paw. "Yes!"

A long line of undulating darkness passed between them and the surface, turned, and passed again a little closer.

"Okay, problems. Plural. I need the tooth to close the hole."

"Great." Sam kept his eyes on the serpent, now one pass closer. "So call it."

Diana reached out and grabbed him as the lashing of his tail propelled him upwards. "Two problems with that. One, it might be locked away and not able to move freely, and, two, we don't know how far away it is. Staying down here indefinitely is really not an option. We need to go to it."

"And?"

"And that's not a problem: given that we've got the rest of the jaw, we'll just follow it. The problem is, I can't pull from the Possibilities this close to the hole."

"So we leave and come back another day. And when I say we come back," Sam amended, as he wriggled free and started swimming toward shore, "I mean you."

Diana grabbed him again. "Did I mention that the serpent has to go back through the hole before I close it? If we leave and come back, the serpent could be anywhere, not to mention that another serpent—or worse—could come through."

"You're just full of good news."

"But, I have a plan."

"Oh, joy."

"You won't like it."

He sighed. "Why am I not surprised?"

"I'm going to use the Possibilities that are keeping us dry and breathing."

"There's a problem with that." He squirmed around until he looked her in the face. "They're keeping us dry and breathing."

"We take a deep breath, and the next instant we'll be standing by the missing tooth."

"That doesn't sound so bad."

"We'll just be a little wet."

"When you say a little, you mean..."

"Completely."

He locked his claws in her jacket. "No."

"Would you rather be eaten by the lake monster?"

Sam glanced toward the surface. The serpent was close

enough that Diana could see the broad band of lighter-brown scales around its neck. It seemed to be picking up speed with each pass, confidence growing as nothing opposed it.

"Sam?"

"I'm thinking."

There were teeth visible just inside the broad mouth. Rather too many teeth, in Diana's opinion. Rather too many teeth suddenly facing them. And closing fast. Really, really fast. "Take a deep breath, Sam."

"I don't..."

"Now!"

And they were standing, dripping, in a basement workshop, the room barely lit by two low windows.

"I'm wet!" Claws breaking through denim to skin, Sam leapt out of Diana's arms and raced around the room, spraying water from his sodden fur. "Wet! Wet! Ahhhhh! Wet!" Tail clamped tight to his body, he disappeared under the lower shelf of the workbench.

"Oh for..." Far enough from the hole that all Possibilities were open to her, Diana reached. "There. Now, you're dry."

"I'm still sitting in a puddle," came a disgruntled voice from under the bench.

"So move." Taking her own advice, Diana stepped out of a puddle of her own and held out the jaw. "Can you hear that?"

"I have water in my ears."

"Sam!"

"Fine." He crawled out from under the bench, shook, and sat, head cocked. "I hear tapping."

"Can you find it?"

The look he shot her promised dire consequences.

"I'm sorry. *Would* you find it? Please." Not a compulsion, just a polite request. Compelling cats had much the same success rate as Senate reform, which was to say, none at all.

The tooth was in a small plastic box, tucked inside a red, metal tool box, shoved to the back of an upper shelf.

"What's the point of having a souvenir no one can see?" Sam wondered as the tooth settled back into the jaw with an audible click.

"I guess the point's having it. Let's go."

"In a minute." He walked over to where a full wet suit hung on the wall, neoprene booties lined up neatly under it. Tail held high, he turned around.

"What are you doing?"

He looked up at her like she was an idiot. In fairness, it was a stupid question.

"Good aim," she acknowledged when he finished. "I just hope they don't have a cat that can be blamed when he puts that boot on next."

"They don't."

"You really got upset about him taking that tooth," she murmured, bending and scooping him up.

"Please," he snorted, settling into the crook of her arm. "I got *wet!*"

"Who are you?"

She stared at Sam, who shrugged in an unhelpful manner, then turned toward the piping voice.

A little girl, no more than five, stood in the open doorway, half hanging off the door knob. Behind her, a rec room; empty but for a scattering of brightly-coloured toys.

Diana glanced down at the jaw and smiled. "I'm the tooth

fairy," she said, reached into the Possibilities, and allowed the bone to pull them back to the wreck.

The serpent was nowhere in sight, but since they hadn't been gone long, she figured it hadn't gone far. The trick would be getting it to come back.

"Sam! What are you doing?"

He paused, up on his hind legs, front claws embedded in a squared piece of timber. "Is that a trick question?"

"Just stop it."

"Fine." Sighing, he swam back over beside her. "Now what?"

"We need to lure the serpent back through the hole before I can close it."

"I refuse to be bait."

"I wasn't going to ask."

"Good."

She nodded at the lone herring watching from the shelter of the wreck. "I need you to talk to your friend."

"It's a fish."

"So?"

"It's not a friend, it's food."

"So you can't talk to it."

Whiskers bristled indignantly. "I didn't say that!"

"I need you to ask it to get a school together, get the serpent's attention, lure it back here, and peel away at the last minute so that the serpent goes through the hole rather than hitting the rock."

Sam stared at her. "You want me to convince fish to be bait? Why don't I just convince them to roll in breadcrumbs and lie down under a broiler?" The darker orange markings on his forehead formed a 'w' as he frowned. "Actually, that's not a bad idea."

"If they do this, the serpent will be gone, and they'll be a lot safer."

"Provided he doesn't catch them and eat them."

"I'm not saying there isn't a risk. Just try."

As Sam swam over to the herring, Diana slid her backpack around onto her lap and undid the zipper. She needed something that would write under water on slippery, algae-covered rock. Pens, pencils, markers, bag of biodegradable kitty litter, litter box, six cans of cat food, two cat dishes, box of crackers, peanut butter, pyjamas, clean jeans, socks, underwear, laptop; nothing that would work. The outside pockets held her cellphone, a bottle of slightly redundant water, and... a nail file. Possibly...

"She wants you to sweeten the deal."

"She does?" Diana glanced over at the herring. "How?"

"She wants you to get rid of the fish that suck the life out of other fish."

"There's vampire fish in this lake?" All at once, the dark corners under the rocks looked a little darker.

"Get real. They're called sea lampreys. They came into the lake after World War II and decimated the native populations. TVO special on the Great Lakes," he added when Diana blinked at him.

"Decimated?"

"It means ate most of."

"I *know* what it means."

"Hey, you asked," he snorted. "What do you say? They're not supposed to be here, no one would miss them, and you can't lure the serpent without herring co-operation. She just wants her fry to be safe." He paused and licked his lips.

"You're thinking about fried fish, aren't you?"

"Yeah."

"Well, stop." If she gave the herring what she wanted, Diana knew there'd be consequences. More healthy, native species of fish in the lake, for one thing. Actually, more healthy, native species of fish in the lake was about the only thing. She couldn't see a down side—which was always vaguely unsettling.

"You can't do it, can you?"

"Of course I can do it." It was disconcerting that her cat was using the same argument on her that she'd used on him. "Technically, as a Keeper, if I'm asked for help to right a wrong, I can't refuse. Sea lampreys in the lake seem to be definitely a wrong."

"So what's the problem?"

"I'm not sure fish were included under that rule."

"Very anti-ichthyoid of you."

"Anti what? Never mind." She waved off his explanation. "You're watching way too much television. Okay, tell her I'll do it, but it has to be after the hole is closed, I can't access the Possibilities until then."

"She wants to know why she should trust you."

Diana glanced over at the herring. "Because I'm one of the good guys."

"She only has your word for that."

"Sam!"

"Okay, okay, she didn't say that. You get to work; I'll convince her you're trustworthy."

"Thank you." Setting the jaw bone carefully aside, Diana began to scratch the definitions of the accident site onto the rocks around the hole with the point of her nail file, the algae just thick enough for it to leave a legible impression.

"Incoming!"

"I'm almost done."

"Maybe you don't quite understand what incoming means," Sam shouted as the first herring whacked into her shoulder.

Diana scrambled to get the last definition drawn in the midst of a silver swirl of fish and dove out of the way in the instant of clear water that followed.

Given a choice between diving face first into rock or returning back where it had come from, the serpent chose the second, less painful, option.

The instant the tip of its wedge-shaped tail disappeared, Diana grabbed the definitions and slammed the hole closed. When she looked up, three dozen silver faces stared back at her, all wearing the same expectant expression. Well, probably expectant; it was surprisingly hard to judge expression on a fish.

"Okay, okay, give me a minute to catch my breath." She tested the seal on the hole and reached into the Possibilities. Turned out there were a lot of sea lamprey in the lake, and over half of them had to be removed from living prey.

"Where'd you put them?" Sam spun around in a slow circle, lazily sculling with his tail.

"I dropped them in the Mid-Atlantic."

"There are sharks in the Mid-Atlantic."

"So?"

"Sharks eat lampreys."

"Sharks eat Volkswagens. What's your point?"

"We've been down here for hours, we missed lunch, and I'm hungry. Can we go now?"

"In a minute, I have one more thing to do."

It was only a part of a jaw bone, but once it had been a part of a man who'd sailed the lakes.

Diana set the bone down beside the wreck and waited.

He hadn't been very old. Under his knit cap, his hair was brown, long enough to wisp out over his ears, and there was a glint of red in his bad teenage moustache. He wore faded blue pants with a patch on one knee. His heavy sweater looked a little too big for him, but that may have been because he was wearing it over at least one other sweater, maybe two. At some point, not long before he'd died, he'd whacked the index finger on his left hand, leaving the nail black and blue.

Pulling the two copper coins from her pocket, Diana bent and laid one on each closed eye. "To pay the ferryman," she said, feeling Sam's unasked question. "He's been in the water long enough, I think he'd like to be back on it."

A heartbeat later, there was only the wreck and the rocks.

The coins and the jaw bone were gone.

"Now, can we go?"

Diana slung her backpack over one shoulder and picked up the cat with her other hand. "Yes. Now we can go."

Carol Diamond was standing on the shore when she came out of the water. Her eyes were wide and her mouth worked for a moment before any sound emerged. "You went... you were... in the..."

"I went wading."

"Wading?"

"Yes. You saw me wading. Then I came out of the water..." Diana stepped over the ridge of zebra mussel shells and set Sam down on the gravel. "...and I rolled down my jeans and put my shoes and socks back on."

White curls bounced as she shook her head. "You were under the water!"

"Couldn't have been. I'm completely dry."

"But you..."

"But I what?" Diana held the older woman's gaze.

"You went wading?"

"Yes, I did."

"But that water must be freezing!"

"I hardly felt it."

"Well," Carol laughed a little uncertainly, "it must be nice to be young. Doesn't that rock look just like an orange cat?"

"You think? I don't see it."

Sam sighed and headed for the dock.

🐾

Ryan sat between the two girls on the way back to the mainland. There was a fair bit of giggling from all concerned.

The lake was calm, the silvered blue broken only by the wake of the boat and a small school of herring rising to feed on the water bugs dimpling the surface.

Sam had eaten, then curled up and gone to sleep in her backpack. Dangling a bottle of water from one hand, Diana leaned back against the gunnels and listened to Gary Straum list just some of the more than fifty ships that had gone down between Point Petre and Main Duck Island. She didn't know which ship her sailor had been from, but it didn't really matter.

He was home now.

"The Metcalfe, the Maggie Hunter, the Gazelle, the Norway, the Atlas, the Annie Falconer, the Olive Branch, the Sheboygan, the Ida Walker, the Maple Glenn, the Lady Washington..."

When asked to write a story for Katherine Kurtz and The Tales of the Knights Templar, I devoured every bit of information on the Knights Templar I could find. And still missed a bit, having to add jewels to the medallion in later versions of the story to fit the new information Katherine had included in her afterword. In that afterword, she also mentioned that the splinter was believed to be one of the hallows that fell into the hands of Philip of France. Given the demands of the story, I chose not to believe it and Katherine kindly allowed my version to stand.

This story makes me cry every time I read it. I don't think anything else I've written has that strong an effect.

WORD OF HONOUR

The prayer became a background drone without words, without meaning, holding no relevance to her life even had she bothered to listen.

Pat Tarrill shoved her hands deep in her jacket pockets and wondered why she'd come. The moment she'd read about it in the paper, attending the Culloden Memorial Ceremony had become an itch she had to scratch—although it wasn't the sort of thing she'd normally waste her time at. *And that's exactly what I'm doing. Wasting time.* Sometimes, she felt like that was all she'd been doing the entire twenty-five years of her life. Wasting time.

The prayer ended. Pat looked up, squinted against the wind blowing in off Northumberland Strait, and locked eyes with a wizened old man in a wheelchair. She scowled and stepped forward, but lost sight of him as the bodies around the cairn shifted position. Probably just another dirty old man, she thought, closed her eyes and lost herself in the wail of the pipes.

Later, while everyone else hurried off to the banquet laid out in St. Mary's Church hall, Pat walked slowly to the cairn and lightly touched the damp stain. Raising her fingers to her face, she sniffed the residue and smiled, once again hearing her grandfather grumble that, *"No true Scot would waste whiskey on a rock."* But her grandfather had been dead for years and the family had left old Scotland for Nova Scotia in 1770.

Wiping her fingers on her jeans, Pat headed for her car. She hadn't been able to afford a ticket to the banquet and wouldn't have gone even if she could have. All that Scots wha hae stuff made her nauseous.

"Especially," she muttered, digging for her keys, "since most of this lot has been no closer to Scotland than Glace Bay."

With one hand on the pitted handle of her car door, she froze, then slowly turned, pulled around by the certain knowledge she was being observed. It was the old man again, sitting in his chair at the edge of the church yard, staring in her direction. This time, a tall, pale man in a tan overcoat stood behind him—also staring. Staring down his nose, Pat corrected. Even at that distance the younger man's attitude was blatantly obvious. Flipping the two of them the finger, she slid into her car.

She caught one last glimpse of them in the rear view mirror as she peeled out of the gravel parking lot. Tall and pale appeared to be arguing with the old man.

"Patricia Tarrill?"

"Pat Tarrill. Yeah."

"I'm Harris MacClery, Mr. Hardie's solicitor."

Tucking the receiver between ear and shoulder, Pat forced her right foot into a cowboy boot. "So, should I know you?"

"I'm Mr. Chalmer Hardie's solicitor."

"Oh." Everyone in Atlantic Canada knew of Chalmer Hardie. He owned... well, he owned a good chunk of Atlantic Canada.

"Mr. Hardie would like to speak with you."

"With me?" Her voice rose to an undignified squeak. "What about?"

"A job."

Pat's gaze pivoted toward the stack of unpaid bills threatening to bury the phone. She'd been unemployed for a month and the last job hadn't lasted long enough for her to qualify for Unemployment Insurance. "I'll take it."

"Don't you want to know what it's about?"

She could hear his disapproval and, frankly, she didn't give two shits. Anything would be better than yet another visit to the welfare office. "No," she told him, "I don't."

As she scribbled directions on the back of an envelope, she wondered if her luck had finally changed.

❃

Chalmer Hardie lived in Dunmaglass, a hamlet tucked between Baileys Brook and Lismore, the village where the Culloden Memorial had taken place. More specifically, Chalmer Hardie *was* Dunmaglass. Tucked up against the road was a gas station/general store/post office and up a long lane was the biggest house Pat had ever seen.

She swore softly in awe as she parked the car then swore again as a tall, pale man came out of the house to meet her.

"Ms. Tarrill." It wasn't a question, but then, he knew what she looked like. "Mr. Hardie is waiting."

"Ms. Tarrill." The old man in the wheelchair held out his hand. "I'm very happy to meet you."

"Um, me too. That is, I'm happy to meet you." His hand felt dry and soft, and although his fingers curved around hers, they didn't grip. Up close, his skin was pale yellow and it hung off his skull in loose folds, falling into accordion pleats around his neck.

"Please forgive me if we go directly to business." He waved her toward a brocade wing chair. "I dislike wasting the little time I have left."

Pat lowered herself into the chair feeling as if she should've worn a skirt and resenting the feeling.

"I have a commission I wish you to fulfil for me, Ms. Tarrill." Eyes locked on hers, Chalmer Hardie folded his hands over a small wooden box resting on his lap. "In return, you will receive ten thousand dollars and a position in one of my companies."

"A position?"

"A job, Ms. Tarrill."

"And ten thousand dollars?"

"That is correct."

"So, who do you want me to kill?" She regretted it almost instantly, but the richest man in the Maritimes merely shook his head.

"I'm afraid he's already dead." The old man's fingers tightened around the box. "I want you to return something to him."

"Him who?"

"Alexander MacGillivray. He lead Clan Chattan at Culloden as the chief was, at the time, a member of the Black Watch and thus not in a position to support the prince."

"I know."

Sparse white eyebrows rose. "You know?"

Pat shrugged. "My grandfather was big into all that..." She paused and searched for an alternative to *Scottish history crap.* "...heritage stuff."

"I see. Would it be too much to ask that he ever mentioned the Knights Templar?"

He'd once gotten into a drunken fight with a Knight of Columbus... "Yeah, it would."

"Then I'm afraid we'll have to include a short history lesson or none of this will make sense."

For ten thousand bucks and job, Pat could care less if it made sense, but she arranged her face into what she hoped was an interested expression and waited.

Frowning slightly, Hardie thought for a moment. When he began to speak, his voice took on the cadences of a lecture hall. "The Knights Templar were a brotherhood of fighting monks sworn to defend the holy land of the Bible from the infidel. In 1132, the patriarch of Jerusalem gave Hugh de Payens, the first Master of the Knights, a relic, a splinter of the True Cross sealed into a small crystal orb that could be worn like a medallion. This medallion was to protect the master and through his leadership, the holy knights.

"In 1307, King Philip of France, for reasons we haven't time to go into, decided to destroy the Templars. He convinced the current Grand Master, Philip de Molay, to come to France, planning to arrest him and all the Templars in the country in one fell swoop. Which he did. They were tortured, and many of them, including their Master, were burned alive as heretics."

"Wait a minute," Pat protested, leaning forward. "I thought the medallion thing was supposed to protect them?"

Hardie grimaced. "Yes, well, a very short time before they were arrested, de Molay was warned. He sent a messenger with the medallion to the Templar Fleet with orders for them to put out to sea."

"If he was warned, why didn't he run himself?"

"Because that would not have been the honourable thing to do."

"Like dying's so honourable." She bit her lip and wished that just once her brain would work before her mouth.

The old man stared at her for a long moment then continued as though she hadn't expressed an opinion. "While de Molay believed that nothing would happen to him personally, he had a strong and accurate suspicion that King Philip was after the Templars' not inconsiderable treasure. Much of that treasure had already been loaded onto the ships of the fleet.

"The fleet landed in Scotland. Maintaining their tradition of service, the Knights became a secular organization and married into the existing Scottish nobility. The treasure the fleet carried was divided amongst the Knights for safekeeping and, as the centuries passed, many pieces became family heirlooms and were passed from father to son.

"Now then, Culloden... In 1745 Bonnie Prince Charlie returned from exile to Scotland and, a year later, suffered a final defeat at Culloden. The clans supporting him were slaughtered. Among the dead were many men of the old Templar families." He opened the box on his lap and beckoned Pat closer.

Resting on a padded red velvet lining was probably the ugliest piece of jewelry she'd ever seen—and as a fan of the home shopping network, she'd seen some ugly jewelry. In the centre of a gold disc about two inches across, patterned with what looked like little specks of gold and inset with coloured stones, was a yellowish and uneven crystal sphere about the size of a marble. A modern gold chain filled the rest of the box.

"An ancestor of mine stole that before the battle from Alexander MacGillivray. You, Ms. Tarrill are looking at an actual sliver of the True Cross."

Squinting, Pat could just barely make out a black speck in the centre of the crystal. Sliver of the True Cross my aunt fanny. "This is what..." She searched her memory for the name and couldn't find it. "...that Templar guy sent out of France?"

"Yes."

"How do you know?"

"Trust me, Ms. Tarrill. I know. I want you to take this holy relic, and place it in the grave of Alexander MacGillivray."

"In Scotland?"

"That is correct. Mr. MacClery will give you the details. I will, of course, pay all expenses."

Pat studied the medallion, lips pursed. "I have another question."

"Perfectly understandable."

"Why me?"

"Because I am too sick to make the journey, and because I

had a dream." His lips twitched into a half smile as though he realized how ridiculous he sounded but didn't care. "I dreamt about a young woman beside the cairn at the Culloden Memorial Ceremony—you, Ms. Tarrill."

"You're going to trust me with this, give me ten thousand bucks and a job based on a dream?"

"You don't understand." One finger lightly touched the crystal. "But you will."

As crazy as it sounded, he seemed to believe it. "Did the dream give you my name?"

"No. Mr. MacClery had your license plate traced."

Her eyes narrowed. Lawyers! "So, why do you want this thing returned? I mean, if it was supposed to protect MacGillivray and Clan Chattan at Culloden giving it back isn't going to change the fact that the Duke of Cumberland kicked butt."

"I don't want to change things, Ms. Tarrill. I want to do what's right." His chin lifted and she saw the effort that small movement needed. "I have been dying for a long time; time enough to develop a conscience, if you will. I want the cross of Christ back where it belongs and I want you to take it there." His shoulders slumped. "I would rather go myself, but I left it too long."

Pat glanced toward the door and wondered if lawyers listened through keyholes. "Is Mr. MacClery going with me?"

"No. You'll go alone."

"Then what proof do you want that I actually put it in the grave?"

"Your word will be sufficient."

"My word? That's it?"

"Yes."

She could tell from his expression that he truly believed her word would be enough. Wondering how anyone so gullible had gotten so rich, she gave it.

Pat had never been up in a plane before and, as much as she'd intended to be cool about it, she kept her face pressed against the window until the lights of St. John's were replaced by the featureless black of the North Atlantic. In her purse, safe under her left arm, she carried the boxed medallion and a hefty packet of money MacClery had given her just before she boarded.

Although it was an overnight flight, Pat didn't expect to sleep; she was too excited. But the food was awful and she'd seen the movie and soon staying awake became more trouble than it was worth.

A few moments later, wondering grumpily who'd play the bagpipes on an aeroplane, she opened her eyes.

Instead of the blue tweed of the seat in front of her, she was looking down at an attractive young man—tall and muscular, red-gold hair above delicate dark brows and long, thick lashes. At the moment he needed a shave and a bath, but she still wouldn't kick him out of bed for eating crackers. A hand, with rather a great quantity of black hair growing across the back of it, reached down and shook the young man's shoulder. With a bit of a shock, she realized the hand was hers. *Well, this dream's probably not heading where I'd like it to...*

"Alex! Get your great lazy carcass on its feet. There's a battle to be fought." Her mouth formed the words, but she had no control over either content or delivery. It appeared she was merely a passenger.

Grey eyes snapped open. "Davie? I must've dozed off..."

"You fell asleep, but there's no crime in that. Lord John is with his Highness in Culloden House and Cumberland's men are up and about."

"Aye, then so should I be." Shaking his head to clear the sleep from it, Alexander MacGillivray, lieutenant-colonel of Clan Chattan heaved himself up onto his feet, his right hand moving to touch his breast as he stood.

His fair skin went paler still and his eyes widened so far they must've hurt. He dug under his clothing then whirled about to search the place he'd lain.

"What is it, Alex? Have you lost something?" Pat felt Davie's heart begin to race and over it, pressed hard against his skin, she felt a warm weight hanging. All at once, she knew it had to be the medallion and that meant Davie had to be Davie Hardie, Chalmer Hardie's ancestor. Stuffed into Hardie's head, she could access what it held; he'd known the medallion had been in the MacGillivray family for a very long time, but had only recently discovered what it was. More a scholar than a soldier, he'd found a reference to it in an old manuscript, had tracked it back to the Templar landing in Argyll where the MacGillivrays originated, had combed the scraps of Templar history that remained, and had discovered what it held and the power attributed to it. He hadn't intended to take advantage of what he'd found—and then Charles Edward Stuart and war had come to Scotland.

Pat could feel Davie Hardie's fear of facing Cumberland's army and touched the memory of how he'd stolen the medallion's protection for himself, even though he'd known that if it were worn by one with the right it could very well protect the entire clan. *That cowardly son of a bitch!*

When Alexander MacGillivray straightened, Pat could read his thoughts off his face. By losing the medallion, he'd betrayed a sacred trust. There was only one thing he could do.

"Alex?"

The young commander squared his shoulders, faced his own death, and tugged on his bonnet. "Come along, Davie. I need to talk to the chiefs before we take our place in line."

You need to talk to your pal Davie, that's what you need to do! Then the dream twisted sideways and she winced as a gust of sleet and rain whipped into her face. The Duke of Cumberland's army was a red blot on the moor no more than 500 yards away. When Hardie turned, she saw MacGillivray. When he turned a little further, she could see the companies in line.

Then the first gun boomed across the moor and Hardie whirled in time to see the smoke. A heartbeat later, there was nothing to see but smoke and nothing to hear but screaming.

I don't want to be here! Pat struggled to free herself from the dream. Her terror and Hardie's became one terror. Dream or not, she wanted to die no less than he did.

The cannonade went on. And on.

Through it all, she saw MacGillivray, striding up and down the ranks of his men, giving them courage to stand. Sons were blown to bits beside their fathers, brothers beside brothers. The shot killed chief and humblie indiscriminately, but the line held.

And the cannonade went on.

The clansmen were yelling for the order to charge so they could bring their broadswords into play. The order never came.

And the cannonade went on.

"Sword out, Davie. We've taken as much of this as we're going to."

Hardie grabbed his colonel's arm. "Are you mad?" he yelled over the roar of the guns and shrieks of the dying. "It's not your place to give the order!"

"It's not my place to stand here and watch my people slaughtered!"

"Then why fight at all? Even Lord Murray says we're likely to lose!"

All at once, Pat realized why a man only twenty-five had been chosen to lead the clan in the absence of its chief. Something in his expression spoke quietly of strength and courage and responsibility. "We took an oath to fight for the prince."

"We'll all be killed!"

MacGillivray's eyes narrowed. "Then we'll die with honour."

Pat felt Hardie tremble and wonder how much his colonel suspected. "But the prince!"

"This isn't his doing, it's that damned Irishman, O'Sullivan." Spinning on one heel, he scrugged his bonnet down over his brow and made his way back to the centre of the line.

A moment later, Clan Chattan charged forward into the smoke hoarsely yelling "Loch Moy!" and "Dunmaglass!" The pipes screamed the rant until they were handed to a boy and the Piper pulled his sword and charged forward with the rest.

Davie Hardie charged because he had no choice. Pat caught only glimpses of the faces that ran by, faces that wore rage and despair equally mixed. Then she realized that there seemed to be a great many running by as Hardie stumbled and slowed and made a show of advancing without moving forward.

Cumberland's artillery had switched to grape shot. Faintly, over the roar of the big guns, Pat heard the drum roll firing of muskets. Men fell all around him, whole families died, but nothing touched Davie Hardie.

Then through a break in the smoke and the dying, Pat saw a red-gold head reach the front line of English infantry. Swinging his broadsword, MacGillivray plunged through, leapt over the bodies he'd cut down, and was lost in the scarlet coats.

With his cry of "Dunmaglass!" ringing in her ears, Pat woke. She was clutching her purse so tightly that the edges of the box cut into her hands through the vinyl.

"Death before dishonour, my butt," she muttered as she pushed up the window's stiff plastic shade and blinked in the sudden glare of morning sun. That philosophy had got Alexander MacGillivray dead and buried. Davie Hardie had turned dishonour into a long life in the new world. So he'd had to live knowing that his theft had been responsible for the death of his friend; at least he was alive.

Chill out, Pat. It was only a dream. She accepted a cup of coffee from the stewardess and stirred in double sugar, the spoon rattling against the side of the cup. *Dreams don't mean shit.*

But she could still feel Hardie's willingness to do anything rather than die and it left a bad taste in her mouth.

Customs at Glasgow airport passed her through with a cheery good morning and instructions on where to wait for her connecting flight north to Inverness. The tiny commuter plane was a whole new experience.

At Inverness airport, she was met by a ruddy young man

who introduced himself as Gordon Ritchie, Mr. Hardie's driver. After a few moments of exhausted confusion while they settled which Mr. Hardie, he tugged her suitcase from her hand and bundled her into a discrete black sedan.

"It was all arranged over the phone," Gordon explained as he drove toward the A96 and Inverness. "Here I am, at your beck and call until you head back across the pond."

Pat smiled sleepily. "I love the way you talk."

"Beg your pardon, Ms. Tarrill?"

"Never mind, it's a Canadian thing, you wouldn't understand." A large truck passed the car on the wrong side of the road. Heart in her throat, Pat closed her eyes. Although she hadn't intended to sleep, she remembered nothing more until Gordon called out, "We're here, Ms. Tarrill."

Yawning, she peered out the window. "Call me Pat, and where's here?"

"Station Hotel, Academy Street. Mr. Hardie—Mr. Chalmer Hardie, that is, booked you a room here. It's pretty much the best hotel in town..."

He sounded so tentative that she laughed. "Trust me, you're not the only one wondering if Mr. Hardie knows what he's doing." She could just see herself in some swanky Scottish hotel. *Likely get tossed out for not rolling my r's.*

Her room held a double bed, an overstuffed chair, a small desk spread with tourist brochures, and a chest of drawers. There was a kettle, a china tea pot and two cups on a tray next to a colour TV and a bathroom with both a tub and shower.

"Looks like Mr. Hardie blew the wad." Pat dragged herself as far as the bed and collapsed. After a moment, she pulled the box out of her purse, flipped it open, and stared down at the medallion. It looked the same as it had on the other side of the Atlantic.

"Well, why wouldn't it?" Setting the open box on the bedside table, she stripped and crawled between the sheets. Although it was still early, she'd been travelling for twenty-four hours and was ready to call it a night.

"Bernard? Is that you?"

Who the hell is Bernard? Yanked back to consciousness, Pat opened her eyes and found herself peering down into the bearded face of a burly man standing in the centre of a small boat. The combination of dead fish, salt water, and rotting sewage smelled a lot like Halifax harbour.

"Quiet, Robert," she heard herself say. "Do you want to wake all of Harfleur?"

I guess I'm Bernard. She felt the familiar weight resting on his chest. Oh no, what now? She searched through the young man's memories and found enough references to hear Chalmer Hardie's voice say, *"In 1307 King Philip of France decided to destroy the Templars."*

Pat tried unsuccessfully to wake up. *First Culloden, now this! Why can't I dream about sex, like a normal person?*

The wooden rungs damp and punky under calloused palms, Bernard scrambled down a rickety ladder and joined the man in the boat. Both wore the red Templar cross on a dark brown mantle. They were sergeants, men-at-arms, Pat discovered delving into Bernard's memories again, permitted to serve the order though they weren't nobly born. Bernard had served for only a few short months and his oaths still burned brightly behind every conscious thought.

"I will suffer all that is pleasing to God."

How do I come up with this stuff? She looked over Robert's shoulder and saw, in the grey light of pre-dawn, the eighteen galleys of the Templar Fleet riding at anchor in the harbour.

Covered in road dirt and breathing heavily, Bernard grabbed for support as the boat rocked beneath the two men. "I've come from the Grand Master himself. He said to tell the Preceptor of France that it is time and that he gives this holy relic into his charge."

The crystal orb in the centre of the medallion seemed to gather up what little light there was and Pat could feel the young man's astonished pride at being chosen to bear it.

Over the soft slap, slap of the water against the pilings came the heavy tread of armed men.

Scrambling back up the ladder, Bernard peered over the edge of the dock and muttered, "The seneschal!" in such a tone that Pat heard, *"The cops!"*

Right, let's get out of here.

Chalmer Hardie's voice murmured, *"...burned alive as heretics."*

To her surprise, Bernard raised the medallion to his lips, kissed it devoutly, turned, and dropped the heavy chain over Robert's head.

Pat's point of view shifted radically and her stomach shifted with it.

"Row like you've never rowed before," Bernard told his companion. "I'll delay them as long as I can."

If they close the harbour, the fleet will be trapped. It was Robert's thought, not hers. Hers went more like: *He's going to get himself killed! There's five guys on that wharf! Bernard, get in the damned boat!*

Deftly sliding the oars into the locks, Robert echoed her cry. "Get in the boat. We can both..."

"No." Bernard's gaze measured the distance from the dock to the fleet and the fleet to the harbour mouth. "Wait until I engage before moving clear. They'll have crossbows."

Then Pat remembered Davie Hardie. *Put the medallion back on, you idiot. It'll protect you!*

But this time Robert said only, "Go with God, Brother."

A calm smile flashed in the depths of the young Templar's beard.

You know what the medallion can do! she screamed at him. *So the fleet leaves without it; so what? Is getting it on that boat more important than your life?*

Apparently it was.

When the shouting began, followed quickly by the clash of steel against steel, Robert pulled away from the dock with long, silent strokes. As he rowed, he prayed and tried not to envy the other man's opportunity to prove his devotion to the Lord in battle.

The sun had risen and there was light enough to see Bernard keep all five at bay. Every blow he struck, every blow he took, moved the boat and the holy relic that much closer to the Templar flagship. With his blood, with his life, Bernard bought the safety of the fleet.

A ray of sunlight touched his sword and the entire dockside disappeared in a brilliant flash of white-gold light.

Pat threw up an arm to protect her eyes. When the after images faded, she discovered that the sun had indeed risen and that she'd forgotten to close the blinds before she went to bed.

"Shit."

Something cold slithered across her cheek. Her reaction flung her halfway across the room before she realized it was the chain of the medallion. During the night, she'd taken it from its box and returned to sleep with it cupped in her hand.

Moving slowly, she set it carefully back against the red velvet and sank down on the edge of the bed. Wiping damp palms on the sheets, she sucked in a deep breath. "Look, I'm grateful that you seem to be translating these violent little highlights into modern English so that I understand what's going on, but...

"But I'm losing my mind." Scowling, she stomped into the bathroom. "I'm talking to an ugly piece of jewelry. Obviously, Chalmer Hardie's history lesson made an impression. I'm not stupid," she reminded her reflection. "I could take what he told me and fill in the pieces. I mean, I could be making all that stuff up out of old movies, couldn't I?" She closed her eyes for a moment. "And now I'm talking to a mirror. What next, conversations with the toilet?"

She went back into the bedroom and flicked the box shut. "You," she told it, "are more trouble than you're worth."

Worth...

In a country where the biggest tourist draw was history, there had to be a store that sold pieces of the past. Even back in Halifax there were places where a person could buy anything from old family silver to eighteenth century admiral's insignia.

Gordon assumed jet-lag when she called to say she wouldn't need him and Pat didn't bother to correct his assumption. "Mr. Hardie said you might want to rest before you went off to do whatever it is you're doing for him."

"You don't know?"

He laughed. "I assumed you would."

So Chalmer Hardie hadn't set up the driver to spy on her. Why settle for ten thousand and a job when she could have ten thousand, a job, and whatever the medallion would bring? No one would ever know and Mr. Hardie could die happy, believing she'd been fool enough to stuff it into MacGillivray's grave. With the medallion shoved into the bottom of her purse, Pat headed out into Inverness.

She found what she was searching for on High Street, where shops ranged from authentic Highland to blatant kitsch, all determined to separate tourists from their money. The crowded window of Neal's Curios held several World War II medals, a tea set that was obviously regimental silver although Pat couldn't read the engraving under the raised crest, and an ornate chalice that she'd seen a twin of in *Indiana Jones and the Last Crusade.*

An old ship's bell rang as she pushed open the door and stepped into the shop. The middle aged woman behind the counter put down her book and favoured her with a dazzling smile. "And how may we help you taday, lassie?"

"Are you the owner?"

"Aye. Mrs. Neal, that's me."

"Do you buy old things?"

The smile faded and most of the accent went with it. "Sometimes."

"How much would you give me for this?" Pat dug the box out of her purse and opened it on the scratched glass counter.

Mrs. Neal's pale eyes widened as she peered at the medallion.

"There's a piece of the True Cross in the crystal."

The older woman recovered her poise. "Dearie, if you laid all the so called pieces of the True Cross end to end you could circle the earth at the equator. Twice."

"But this piece comes with a history..."

"Have you any proof?" Mrs. Neal asked when Pat finished embroidering the story Chalmer Hardie had told her. Both her hands were flat on the counter and she leaned forward expectantly.

"Trust me," the old man said. "I know."

Pat sighed. "No. No, proof."

It wasn't exactly a snort of disbelief. "Then I'll give you five hundred pounds for it, but that's mostly for the gold and the gem stones. I can't pay for the fairy tale."

At the current exchange rate, five hundred pounds came to over a thousand dollars. Pat drummed her fingers lightly on the counter while she thought about it. It was less than what she'd expected to get, but she could use the money and Alexander MacGillivray certainly couldn't use the medallion. She opened her mouth to agree to the sale and closed it on air. In the glass cabinet, directly below her fingertips, was a red-enamelled cross about three inches long, all four ends slightly flared. Except for the size, it could have been the cross on the mantle of a Templar sergeant who fought and died to protect the medallion she was about to sell.

Unable to stop her hand from shaking, she picked up the box and shoved it back into her purse. She managed to stammer out that she'd like to think about the offer then turned and nearly ran from the shop.

Before the door had fully closed, Mrs. Neal half-turned and bellowed, "Andrew!"

The scrawny young man who hurried in from the storeroom looked annoyed about the summons. "What is it, Gran? I was having a bit of a kip."

"You can sleep later, I've a job for you." She grabbed his elbow and hustled him over to the door. "See that grey jacket scurrying away? Follow the young woman wearing it and, when you're sure you won't be caught, grab her purse."

"What's in it?"

"A piece of very old jewelry your Gran took a liking to. Now go." She pushed him out onto the sidewalk and watched while he slouched up the street. When both her grandson and the young woman disappeared from sight, she returned to her place behind the counter and slid a box of papers off an overloaded shelf. After a moment's search, she smoothed a faint photocopy of a magazine article out on the counter. The article had speculated about the possibility of the Templar fleet having landed in Argyll and had then gone on to list some of the treasure it might have carried. One page held a sketch of a jewel encrusted, gold medallion that surrounded a marble sized piece of crystal that was reputed to contain a sliver of the True Cross.

Mrs. Neal smiled happily. She knew any number of people who would pay a great deal of money for such a relic without asking uncomfortable questions about how she'd found it.

"I don't believe in signs." Pat threw the box down onto the bed and the medallion spilled out. She paced across the room and back. "I don't believe in you either. You're a fairy tale, just like Mrs. Neal said. The delusions of a dying old man. I should have sold you. I will sell you."

But she left both box and medallion on the bed and spent the afternoon staring at soccer on television. When the game ended, she ordered room service and spent the evening watching programs she didn't understand.

At eleven, Pat put the medallion back in the box, wrapped the box in a shirt and stuffed the bundle into the deepest corner of her suitcase.

"I'm going back there tomorrow," she announced defiantly as she turned off the light.

"Tomorrow, his Majesty intends to arrest the entire Order."

What's going on? I don't even remember going to sleep! Pat fought against opening her eyes but they opened anyway. Bernard?

The young sergeant was on one knee at her feet, his expression anger, disbelief, and awe about equally mixed.

I don't want any part of this! Pat could feel the weight of the medallion and knew the old man who wore it as Philip de Molay, the Grand Master of the Knights Templar. *Last Grand Master,* she corrected, but like all the others, he couldn't hear her. She could feel his anger as he told Bernard what would happen at dawn and gave him the message to pass on to the Preceptor of France—who with fifty knights had all but emptied the Paris Temple five days before. She touched de Molay's decision to stay behind lest the king be warned by his absence.

"There will be horses for you between Paris and Harfleur. You must arrive before dawn, do you understand?"

"Yes, Worshipful Master."

De Molay's hands went to the chain about his neck and he lifted the medallion over his head. He closed his eyes and raised it to his lips, much as Bernard had done. *Would do,* Pat amended. "Take this also to the Preceptor, tell him I give it into his charge." He gazed down into the young sergeant's eyes. "In the crystal is a sliver from the Cross of our Lord. I would not have it fall into the hands of that jackal..." Biting off what would have become an extensive tirade against the king, he held out the medallion. "It will protect you as you ride."

Bernard leaned forward and pressed his lips against the gold. As the Grand Master settled the chain over his head, Pat—who settled into his head—thought he was going to pass out. "Worshipful Master, I am not worthy..."

"I will say who is worthy," de Molay snapped.

"Yes, Worshipful Master." Looking up into de Molay's face through Bernard's lowered lashes, Pat was reminded of her grandfather. *He's a stubborn old man. Certain he's right, regardless of the evidence.* And he was going to die. And there was nothing she could do about it. *Because he died over six hundred years ago,* she told herself. *Get a grip.*

Given the way Bernard had died—would die—Pat expected to hear him declare that he would guard the medallion with his life, but then she realized there was no need, that it was understood. *I don't believe these guys. One of them's staying behind to die, and one of them's riding off to die and neither of them has to!*

If de Molay had left Paris with the rest...

If Bernard had got in the boat...

If MacGillivray had refused to charge...

She woke up furious at the world.

A long, hot shower did little to help and breakfast sat like a rock in her stomach.

"You're worth five hundred pounds to me," she snarled as she crammed shirt, box, and medallion into her purse. "That's all. Five hundred pounds. One thousand..."

Her heart slammed up into her throat as the phone shattered the morning into little pieces. "What?"

"It's Gordon Ritchie, Ms. Tarrill. Pat. I'm in the lobby. If you're feeling better, I thought I might show you around..." His voice trailed off. "Is this a bad time?"

"No. No, it's not." This was exactly what she needed. Something to take her mind off the medallion.

"So where are we going?"

"Well, when he hired me, Mr. Hardie suggested I might take you to Culloden Moor." Gordon held open the lobby door. "The National Trust for Scotland's visitor centre just reopened for the season."

Culloden? Pat ground her teeth. Been there. Done that.

Catching a glimpse of her expression, Gordon frowned. "I could take you somewhere else..."

"No." She cut him off. "Might just as well go along with Mr. Hardie's suggestion. He's paying the bills." Although she was beginning to believe he might not be calling the tune. *Yeah right. As I've said before, Pat, get a grip.*

Swearing under his breath, Andrew ran for his car. At least this morning, his gran'd be willing to front him the money for petrol.

A cold wind was blowing across the moor when they reached the visitor centre. Pat hunched her shoulders, shoved her hands deep into her pockets, and tried not to remember her dream of the slaughter. She watched the presentation, poked around old Leanach Cottage, then started down the path that ran out onto the battlefield, Gordon trailing along behind. She passed the English Stone without pausing, continued west, and came to a roughly triangular, weather-beaten monument.

"'Well of the Dead.'" Her fingers traced the inscription as she read. "'Here the Chief of the MacGillivrays fell.'"

The wind slapped rain into her face. Over the call of the pipes, Pat heard the guns and men screaming and one voice gathering up the clan to aim it at the enemy. *"Dunmaglass!"*

"Pat? Are you all right?"

At Gordon's touch, she shook free of the memory and straightened. "I'd like to go back to the hotel now." He looked so worried that she snarled, "I'm tired, okay?"

He stepped back, quickly masking his reaction, and she wished that just once she'd learn to think before she spoke. He only wanted to help. But she couldn't seem to find the apology she knew he deserved.

"But, Gran!" Andrew protested, raising a hand to protect his head. "It was the only time she even left the bloody hotel, and the guy she had driving her around never left her. Stuck like glue all bloody morning."

Mrs. Neal threw the rolled magazine aside and grabbed her grandson's shirt front. "Then get a couple of your friends and, if you have to, take care of the guy driving her around."

"I could get Colin and Tony. They helped with that bit of silver..."

"I don't care who you get," the old lady spat. "Just bring me that medallion!"

On the way back to the hotel, Pat had Gordon stop and buy her two bottles of cheap scotch. He hadn't approved, she saw it in the set of his shoulders and the thin line of his mouth, but he took the money and came back with the bottles. When she tried to explain, the words got stuck.

Better he thinks I'm a bitch than a lunatic.

She couldn't remember where she'd read that alcohol prevented dreaming and after the first couple of glasses, she didn't care. As afternoon darkened into evening, she curled up in the overstuffed chair and drank herself into a stupor.

"You don't understand, Ms. Tarrill." The old man stroked the crystal lightly with one swollen finger. "But you will."

Before Pat could speak, Chalmer Hardie whirled away; replaced by a progression of scowling old men in offices, ship-yards, and mills all working as though work was all they had. Clothing and surroundings became more and more old fash-ioned and by the time she touched a mind she knew, she realized she was tracing the trail of the medallion back through time.

"Dunmaglass!"

Once again, she watched Alexander MacGillivray lead the charge across Culloden Moor. Then she watched as the Mac-Gillivrays, son to father, returned the clan to Argyll. There were more young men than old in this group for these were men willing to take a stand in a dark time. There were Mac-Gillivrays on the shore when the Templar fleet sailed into Loch Caignish.

"Go with God, Brother."

Bernard smiled and climbed to his death.

"In this crystal is a sliver of the Cross of our Lord. I would not have it fall into the hands of that jackal..."

The Masters of the Knights Templar had not lived easy lives. In spite of the protection of the Cross, many of them died in battle. She saw William de Beaujey, the last Master of the Temple before the Moslems regained the Holy Land, fall defending a breach in the wall of Acre. She saw de Sonnac blinded at Mansourah and de Peragors dying on the sands of Gaza. Master, before Master, before Master, until an old man slipped a medallion over the head of Hugh de Payens.

All at once, Pat could hear pounding and jeers and was suddenly lifted into dim light under an overcast sky. She could see a crowd gathered and a city in the distance but she could feel no one except herself. Then she looked down. The sliver had been taken from near the top of the cross. She saw a crown of thorns, dark hair matted with blood, and the top curve of shoulders marked by a whip.

NO!

For the first time, someone heard her.

Yes.

Tears streaming down her face, Pat woke, still curled in the chair, still clutching the second bottle. When she leapt to her feet, the bottle fell and rolled beneath the bed. She didn't notice. She clawed the box out of her purse, clawed the medallion out of the box, and stared at the crystal.

"All right. That's it. You win." Dragging her nose over her sleeve, she shoved the medallion into one pocket of her jacket, shoved her wallet in the other, and grabbed the phone.

"Gordon? I'm doing what Mr. Hardie wants me to do, now, tonight."

"Ms. Tarrill?"

"Pat. Do you know where the church is in Petty?"

"Sure, my uncle has the parish, but..."

"I'm not drunk." In fact, she'd never felt more sober. "I need to do this." She checked her watch. "It's only just past ten. I'll meet you out front."

She heard him sigh. "I'll be right there."

The car barely had a chance to slow before she flung open the door and threw herself into the passenger seat.

"Ms. Tarrill, I..." He broke off as he caught sight of her face. "Good God, you look terrified. What's wrong?"

Pat found a laugh that didn't mean much. "Good God indeed. I'll tell you later. If I can. Right now, I have something to get rid of."

"And you wanted to call it a night." Andrew let the car get two blocks away then pulled out after it. The large man crammed into the passenger seat of the Mini said nothing and the larger man folded into the back merely grunted.

The church in Petty stood alone on a hill about seven miles east of Inverness, just off the A96. A three-quarter moon and a sky bright with stars sketched out the surrounding graveyard in stark silver and black. Gordon pulled into the driveway and killed the motor.

"At least it's stopped raining," Pat muttered getting out

of the car. "No, you wait here," she added when Gordon attempted to follow. "I have to do this alone."

Lips pressed into a thin line, he dropped into the driver's seat, reclined it back, and pointedly closed his eyes.

Chalmer Hardie's instructions had been clear. *"The MacK-intosh mausoleum is against the west side of the church. Close by it, you'll find a grave stone with only a sword cut into the face. MacGillivray's fiance managed to bury him, but with Cumberland's army squatting in Inverness, she could find no one who dared put his name on the stone. There are MacGillivrays buried in Kilmartin graveyard under similar stones—Templar stones. Put the medallion in the grave."*

Keeping a tight grip on her imagination, Pat found the ancient mausoleum, skirted it, and stared down at the grave of Alexander MacGillivray. Then suddenly realized what put the medallion in the grave meant.

"And me without a shovel." Swallowing hard, she managed to get her stomach under control, although, at the moment, the possibility of spending another night with the medallion frightened her more than a bit of grave digging. She pulled it out of her pocket and glared down at it. All she wanted to do was get rid of it. Why did it have to be so difficult?

"Hand over the jewelry and nobody gets hurt."

Fear clamped both hands around her throat and squeezed her scream into a breathy squeak. When she turned, she saw three substantial shadows between her and the lights that lined Moray Firth. If they were ghosts, Hell provided a pungent aftershave. Two of them were huge. The third was a weasely looking fellow no bigger than she was.

The weasely fellow smiled. "I won't say we don't want to hurt you because me pals here rather like a bit of rough stuff.

Be a smart lady; give it here." While he spoke, the other two closed in.

Pat laughed a bit hysterically. "Look, you have no idea how much I want to get rid of this. Go ahead and..."

Then she stopped. All she could think of was how Davie Hardie had been willing to do anything rather than die.

"Your word will be sufficient."

"My word? That's it?"

"Yes."

She'd given her word that she'd put the medallion in Alexander MacGillivray's grave. Her chin rose and she placed it carefully back in her pocket. "If you want it, you'll have to take it from me."

"You're being stupid."

"Up yours." Pat took a deep breath and was surprised by how calm she felt.

The man on her left jerked forward and she dove to the right. Fingers tangled in her hair, but she twisted free, fell, and scrambled back to her feet. *If I can just get to the car...*

Her ears rang as a fist slid off the side of her head.

A hand clutched the shoulder of her jacket. If she slid out of it they'd have the medallion so she stepped back, driving her heel down onto an instep.

One of them swore and let go. The other wrapped his arm around her neck and hung on. When she struggled, he tightened his grip.

"Right then." The weaselly fellow pinched her cheek, hard.

Pat tried to bite him.

"That'll be enough of tha... ahhhhhhhhh!"

He sounded terrified.

Suddenly free, Pat dropped to her knees. Gasping for

breath, she watched all three of her assailants race away, tripping and stumbling over the gravestones.

"Good... timing... Gordon," she panted, and turned.

It wasn't Gordon.

Alexander MacGillivray had been a tall man, and although it was possible to see the church and the mausoleum through him, death hadn't made him any shorter. Pat looked up. Way up. This time the scream made it through the fear. She stood, stumbled backward into a gravestone and fell. Ghostly fingers reached out towards her...

When she opened her eyes, Pat discovered there was no significant difference between a hospital room in Scotland and one in Canada. They even smelled the same. Ignoring the pain in her head, she pushed herself up onto her elbows and discovered her clothes neatly folded on a chair by the bed.

Teeth clenched, she managed to snag her jacket. Although she half expected the ghost of Alexander MacGillivray to have claimed the medallion, it was still in her pocket. Closing her fingers around it, she stared at the ceiling and thought about what had happened in the graveyard. About what she'd done. About what she hadn't done. About what had sent her there. About the medallion. By the time the nurse came in to check on her, she'd made a decision.

When she fell asleep, she didn't dream.

They'd just cleared the breakfast dishes away—she'd been allowed a glass of juice and hadn't wanted much more—

when Gordon, looking as though he'd spent a sleepless night, stuck his head into the room. When he saw she was awake, he walked over to the bed. "I'm not a relative," he explained self-consciously. "They made me go home."

"The nurse said you nearly drove through the doors at emergency."

"It seemed the least I could do." His expression shifted through worry, relief, and anger. "I came running when I heard the screams. When I saw you on the ground..."

"You didn't see anyone else?"

"No." He frowned. "Should I have?"

If she said she'd been attacked, the police would have to be involved, and what would be the point?

"Pat, what happened?"

"I saw a ghost." She shrugged and wished she hadn't as little explosions went off inside her skull. "I guess I tripped and hit my head."

Scooping her clothes off the chair, he sat down. "I guess you did. The nurse at the desk told me that if you'd hit it two inches lower, you'd be dead." He coloured as she winced. "Sorry."

"S'okay. Gordon, last night you said your uncle had the parish of Petty. Does that mean he's the minister there?"

It took him a moment to get around the sudden change of topic. "Uh, yes."

"Is he a good man?"

"He's a minister!"

"You know what I mean."

Gordon considered it. "Yes," he said after a moment, "he's a good man."

"Could you call him?" Pat lightly stroked the crystal with one finger. "And ask him to come and see me..."

❇

Sunlight brushed the hard angles off the graveyard and softened both the grey of the stones and the red brick of Petty church. Released from the hospital that morning, Pat looked out over the water of Moray Firth then down at the grave of Alexander MacGillivray.

"I gave my word to Chalmer Hardie that I'd put the medallion in your grave." She sighed, and spread her hands. "I don't have it anymore. I tried to call him, but he's in the hospital and MacClery won't let me talk to him. Anyway, I'm going home tomorrow and I thought you deserved an explanation."

When she paused, the silence waited for her to continue. "So many of the Templars died violently that I was confused for a while about the medallion's power to protect. You gave me the clue. If you'd thought it could stop shot, you'd have torn the country apart to find it before you sacrificed the lives of your people. Davie Hardie wanted the medallion to protect him from dying in battle, so that's what it did—but the Templars expected to die in battle, so they wanted protection against the things that would cause them to break their vows." Her cheeks grew hot as she remembered how close to betrayal she personally had come and how much five hundred pounds sounded like thirty pieces of silver. "Chalmer Hardie wanted me to right the wrong his ancestor did you by returning the medallion to where he thought it belonged. But I don't think it belongs with the dead. I think we could really use that kind of protection active in the world right now.

"Gordon's uncle says there's still Templar organizations in Scotland, even after all this time. I thought you'd like to know that." The gravestone was warm under her fingertips as she traced the shallow carving of the sword. "He gave me his word that he'll give it to the person in charge.

"So, I'm bringing you his promise in place of the medallion."

Shoving her hands into her pockets, she turned to go. Then she remembered one more thing. "I could still lie to Mr. Hardie. Tell him you got the medallion back, pick up that ten grand and the job—but I won't. Because it isn't dying honourably that counts, is it? It's living honourably, right to the end."

As she reached the corner of the church and could see Gordon waiting by the car, the hair lifted off the back of her neck. The silence pulled her around.

Standing on the grave was a tall young man with red-gold hair and pale skin, in the clothing of the Jacobite army. Pat forgot to breathe. He hadn't been wearing the medallion the night he'd driven off the three thugs, but today it hung gleaming against his chest.

The air shimmered and she saw a line of men stretch into the distance behind him. They all wore the medallion. Many wore the white mantle and red cross of the Templar Knights. One wore the brown mantle of man-at-arms. For an instant, she felt a familiar weight around her neck, then both the weight and all the shades but Alexander MacGillivray's disappeared.

Tell Chalmer Hardie, he said to her heart as he faded, *that you kept your word.*

ABOUT THE AUTHOR

Although she left Nova Scotia at three, and has lived most of her life since in Ontario, Tanya Huff still considers herself a Maritimer. On the way to the idyllic rural existence she shares with her partner Fiona Patton, six cats, and a Chihuahua, she acquired a degree in Radio and Television Arts from Ryerson Polytechnic—an education she was happy to finally use when writing her SMOKE novels. Of her previous twenty-three books, the five BLOOD novels featuring Henry Fitzroy, a bastard son of Henry VIII, romance writer, and vampire, are among the most popular. In fact these books became so popular that they inspired the TV series, *Blood Ties*.

FOR NEWS ABOUT
JABBERWOCKY
BOOKS AND AUTHORS

Sign up for our newsletter*: http://eepurl.com/b84tDz
visit our website: awfulagent.com/ebooks
or follow us on twitter: @awfulagent

THANKS FOR READING!

*We will never sell or giveaway your email address, nor use
it for nefarious purposes. Newsletter sent out quarterly.

CPSIA information can be obtained
at www.ICGtesting.com
Printed in the USA
LVOW10s1204060817
544020LV00003B/461/P